Lock Down Publications and Ca$h
Presents

HUNGRY FOR MONEY 2

HALFTIME

By

SLIMBOS

First Edition 2024

Printed in the United States of America

Lock Down Publications
P.O. Box 944
Stockbridge, GA 30281
www.lockdownpublications.com

Like our page on Facebook: Lock Down Publications
www.facebook.com/lockdownpublications.ldp

Stay Connected with Us!

Text **LOCKDOWN** to 22828 to stay up-to-date with new releases, sneak peaks, contests and more…

Like our page on Facebook:
Lock Down Publications

Join Lock Down Publications/The New Era Reading Group

Visit our website:
www.lockdownpublications.com

Follow us on Instagram:
Lock Down Publications

Email Us: We want to hear from you!

PROLOGUE

In basketball, each team has twenty-four seconds to shoot the ball. There are four quarters... but halftime is where you huddle up with your teammates and figure out how you're going to end the game. Sometimes, you can make adjustments during halftime that will give you an advantage over your opponents. This was what Rednose implemented, some halftime adjustments.

Everybody thought Cee Money and Rednose were no longer in contact until the end of part one. In part one, 24 Seconds, Rednose and Cee Money played a trick on the entire city. After Rednose confessed that he went too far with the Carlos situation, him and Cee Money had a long discussion. That was when they decided to keep their reunion a secret.

Rednose explained to her that his explosive disorder had reached a new level during the Carlos ordeal. He admitted he became emotional and acted off impulse without thinking. He actually released years of trauma on Carlos for months as he held him hostage before he killed him and hung him on that tree. He used all types of objects to make Carlos feel violated because Carlos and his gang took advantage of young women. Rednose made him suffer in similar ways. Cee Money knew Rednose was crazy, but after he revealed the gruesome details, she knew he was beyond sick. Hey, man, it sounded weird, but somehow, some way, this turned her on and attracted her to him even more. It sounded crazy, but dangerous boys always stole her eye. She couldn't do anything with a soft nigga. If he wasn't tough and hardcore and ready to kill somebody for her, she did not want him.

After Rednose confessed the truth about Carlos, even after she told him to let it go, she decided to be honest about her involvement with the setup. Yes!! Cee Money tried to set Rednose up, and he still took her back. Sounded crazy, didn't it? Well, love made you do crazy things. It seemed like everything happened in twenty-four seconds that night in the apartments. Cee Money actually felt like she had no other choice. It was either her sister or Rednose. She explained to him that "no man came before her family." Rednose respected her for being honest. There were not too many females that would confess that they actually tried to set you up. It was flat out disloyal! However, at the same time, she was being loyal to her blood sister. So, was Cee Money loyal or disloyal?

Furthermore, Cee money also explained to Rednose how the RRG members knew her location when they broke in her house and tried to ambush Rednose. That was because Carlos used to live with her. They were a couple before she even met Rednose, but it was only because Cee Money needed financial stability, and Carlos was one of the richest niggas in the city. Cee Money's mother, Trina, showed her a long time ago how to satisfy her hunger for money.

Ebony and Coby played a trick on Rednose as well, proclaiming to be brother and sister. The truth was that they were not even real siblings. They thought Rednose had no idea. The entire time, they thought they were fooling him, but all along, he was the one fooling them because Cee Money had been put him on point.

Once Cee Money and Rednose squashed their beef, they still had a major issue. The whole city was upset about Carlos' death. In order for Rednose to survive, him and Cee Money decided to finesse the situation. They masqueraded as if they were actually still beefing. However, this was not the case at all because the whole time, Cee Money was reporting everything back to Rednose.

Rednose would go over all the information he received from his ninja, Cee Money, and set up easy targets for his shooter, Coby. Whenever it was sweet and the ops were least expecting it, Rednose would have Coby spin the block on the RRG members. They were able to eliminate most members. When Coby started his own game back in the city, Rednose was the mastermind behind the scenes, calling all the shots. Coby was satisfied with getting all the credit and popularity.

The most difficult task was Carlos' main shooter. Rednose realized that it had become very hard to kill Ice Water. This young nigga was ruthless and very insane. Ice Water was the type of guy that took everything too far. He went the hardest about Carlos' death.

This was when Rednose decided to put Cee Money on him. She played broke and helpless by throwing herself on the tender dick young boy. After she got him to let his guard down, the rest was a piece of cake. She had his nose so wide open that he never saw the day coming when she walked him directly into a death trap. This was how Rednose got the drop on him and was able to take him out so easily. If "Cash" taught us not to TRUST NO MAN, then Cee Money should be a good reason why you should not "trust no bitch!" Ice Water learned the hard way.

By coincidence, Ice Water had also been beefing with Coby because they were in love with the same female. Ice Water had mistakenly shot her to death while shooting at Coby. This moved the beef to a higher level. Rednose really became furious and fed up when Ice Water and the RRG members shot up the house that him, Coby, and Ebony were staying in before they moved out the city.

Their location should have never been available. Coby got emotional during an argument over the phone with Ice Water. Ice Water outsmarted Coby and made him reveal his location, which led to Ebony being shot and hospitalized for several weeks. That was when Rednose decided to leave the city and let things die down. Meanwhile, Cee Money continued to seduce Ice Water.

Ice Water was so slimy that he didn't give a fuck about Cee Money being Carlos' mistress and main squeeze. He couldn't resist a chance of jumping inside her juicy tight pussy. He had been watching her low-key ever since Carlos first began to bring her around. Ice Water fell for the bait like the duck ass nigga he was. That made things much easier for Rednose to set up the final act which led up to the main event, the showdown —_Ice Water's team versus Coby's team.

During all the action, there was a bunch of behind-the-scenes sex going on between the two love birds... Cee Money had a whole baby by Rednose, and nobody knew besides the two new parents. Rednose's mother and sister mainly kept his son while Cee Money and Rednose scammed and plotted in the streets behind the scenes.

They had a crazy love story, but the love they shared was real. Nobody understood but them. Rednose felt like he owed Cee Money loyalty because she held him down. BEFORE he gave back his life sentence. BEFORE she knew he had a chance to come back home. She was on the phone with him every night. She was there with him during the struggle and hardship. She did things for him that not even his mother or sister would do. All his mother and sister did was lie to him and steal from him. Although she tried to set him up after the Carlos situation, she confessed. She overly elaborated to him about her anxiety and problems with fear. She was afraid for her life. Rednose knew he went too far, and he apologized and promised to work on his explosive disorder.

Now that Ice Water was dead, the RRG members had no real muscle or enforcer. Their days were numbered, and their reign at the top was coming to an end. They were no longer the unstoppable force that they used to be. Most of the members were now joining new gangs and switching up because it wasn't popular to be RRG anymore.

That was how motherfuckers were these days. Only loyal to a certain extent. Only loyal when it was beneficial. Only loyal when their team was winning/ Rednose had been betrayed so many times by disloyal women that he was used to it by now. Those were some of the reasons why he decided to give Cee Money another chance. When it was all bad and you were not as popular as you used to be and you didn't have the connections, money, power, and fame, you did some sucka ass shit and switched up on your people. Fake ass niggas thought they were real ones, These days, nobody was loyal. Everybody was hungry for money and hungry for an opportunity to cross the next person for their own selfish gain. This was one reason why Rednose chose remaining loyal to Cee Money. He'd rather deal with the devil he knew than the devil he didn't know. She had been with him since day one of his planning. Therefore, he decided to remain with her. He didn't give a fuck what anybody had to say or how funny they looked at him. He stood on business and his decision. He was going to make her his queen.

What they didn't know was that although the RRG members were no longer a threat like they were in the past, Carlos still had a few people that wanted revenge, and those few people had eyes on Rednose and Cee Money. One of those guys happened to make it out of the showdown alive. He managed to escape the massive shootout while everyone's attention was on Ice Water and Coby.

His name was Devin, and Ice Water was his uncle. He knew he wasn't ready to go to war with a nigga like Rednose just yet. However, he knew that he would get his day, and he would remain patient until then.

Devin had done time in the county jail with Cee Money's brother, and he knew things about Cee Money's family because her brother was addicted to the new drugs which made people extra friendly and talkative. That was an advantage he had. Nobody knew him, and he wasn't really that popular. This was his time, his chance to avenge the death of Carlos and Ice Water.

Devin also saw this as a chance to gain respect in the streets and make a name for himself. That was exactly what he planned to do. He didn't realize he was just another young dummy that failed to understand life was not a game. The streets were no joke!! Once you entered the jungle, it was hard to make it out... Some people never returned.

That day after all those bodies dropped, Devin just barely escaped unnoticed. With all the attention on Ice Water and Coby, nobody saw him run away. Some would say he was a coward for abandoning his team. But he saw the ship sinking and knew it was time to apply self-preservation. Yeah, he left his gang for dead, but he stayed alive so he could come back and kill the opposition. A good run was better than a bad stay.

Devin remembered seeing Rednose and Cee Money drive away, and he decided to go back to the crime scene to see if any of his team members were still alive. When he got back to the spot, he was sad because he knew nobody was alive. There were no survivors. Everybody was dead! Nothing but dead bodies. That was when he decided to leave.

All of a sudden, he heard coughing coming from somebody lying on the ground. Out of fear, he quickly pulled his gun from his hip and looked around, eyes wide. Once he realized there was nobody there to shoot him, he put his gun back up. He was about to leave, and that was when he heard the coughing again.

He quickly began to search for the survivor. It took him several minutes, but he was surprised to see there was one lone survivor, and the survivor wasn't a part of his team. He was shocked because the survivor was bleeding from his head, indicating there was a bullet in his skull. He couldn't believe that the person was still alive with a bullet in his head. Furthermore, he couldn't believe that the person was Coby.

Chapter 1

Sometimes, Rednose would wake up in the middle of the night, suffering from anxiety, drenched in a cold sweat. This was because of the dream he'd just had. The dream was really actually a nightmare that haunted him over and over. Mostly, the dream would be the same each time with slight differences. It felt so real, as if he had an out of body experience and somehow traveled to another realm. Spooky!

Inside the dream, he was back in the same prison cell that he had suffered in for five years on compound restriction during his ten-year sentence. Inside the dream, he was back to square one, back on compound restriction.

Compound restriction was some new model chain gang shit. These new generation prisoners in Georgia had the system fucked up. Officers didn't even have to do any work anymore. These niggas were doing the polices' job. Rednose called them "Inmate Task Squad." The inmates thought they were the cops!!! You had a certain group of inmates who acted as the damn police and would police the dorm. House nigga, field nigga.

Most niggas complied out of fear, or they just didn't want to have any extra drama, but the real ones weren't going for it. So, this caused division and tension in most dorms. If you didn't submit to the new police shit, you were labeled a renegade, and a group of inmate cops forced you into lockdown segregation. Not only was this cruel and unusual, but it also hindered your growth and made your time harder.

It was harder to get access to law library materials to help fight your case, especially if you were one of the ninety percent of lifers housed at Smith State Prison like Rednose was.

Rednose was put off compound by his own gang out of hatred and dislike because he was a natural leader and wasn't going for the bullying and oppression.

During the dreams that randomly haunted him, Rednose was still fighting his life sentence. He was back behind the door in H-2 tier on lockdown segregation with no money or food. Back to dealing with family members stealing his cash and lying to him, making false promises sound believable. Back with nobody to help him! With his back against the wall!! Against all odds... He was subjected to these harsh living conditions for half of his ten-year prison bid. So, to say that he was traumatized was an understatement.

On this particular day, Rednose woke up and immediately looked to his left and began to relax. Next to him was the beautiful Cee Money lying on her side, breathing lightly. She was so damn sexy. The baby only added to her sex appeal. She already had a nice body, but now, she was thick as hell, and her breasts were bigger but still firm, not all saggy. Her newest tattoo read "Rednose's Queen," which was tatted on her neck inside a crown.

"Baby, you need to go get some professional help. I'm serious, nigga, because you are still dealing with a lot of trauma," cried Cee Money in a low and sad voice.

"Huh? What you talking about, bae?" Rednose replied nonchalantly as he tried to play it off by rolling over, so she couldn't see his face.

"Nigga, stop playing with me like I'm stupid! I heard you talking in your sleep, and I know about the dreams! You are still traumatized, and I don't want any more crazy episodes. We have come a long way, and we got a vacation coming soon. Don't ruin my motherfucking trip to the Bahamas with that bipolar shit. You promised if it got worse, you would get some help." Cee Money had caught an attitude now because she knew Rednose was playing on her top.

"Girl, don't start. Shut up and relax, baby, damn. You know it's up when we get to Jamaica! That seven-day cruise going to be exactly what I need to get my mind off all the extra nonsense. I'm alright. I don't need no motherfucking help! Them folks can't tell me anything about me that I don't already know. You tripping." Rednose pulled his queen closer to him.

Cee Money just stared at him for a few seconds before she shook her head then dropped it on his chest. She knew he was stubborn when it came to his mental health. However, she had to stand her ground because of his violent history. Rednose never resulted to violence with her, even after she crossed him. He was so in love with her that he went too far about her. The last nigga's body went viral hanging from a tree, which led to an inner-city war that took place for over a year.

A lot had changed since then between Rednose and Cee Money. They had a son that was going on two years old. Cee Money also had her baby sister, Keisha, living with them ever since she was kidnapped by Coby. Although she wasn't sexually abused, the event still had her shaken up pretty badly. One of her wrists was broken during the shootout when Coby used her body for a shield as Ice Water ran down on him.

Speaking of Ice Water, Cee Money still got goosebumps thinking of how Rednose convinced her to seduce him for months. She tried to get him to trust her without having sex with him, but he wasn't going for that. He not only forced his way in her disrespectfully, but he also fucked her all in her anal, and that shit hurt. He was on the ice, so every time they had sex, it took him over two hours to cum.

Rednose could never catch him slipping because he always fucked her with his Glock in his hand. She was so thrilled the day Rednose was finally able to put him out of his misery. The fact that Ice Water was Carlos' main enforcer made her feel dirty every time he entered her body. If it wasn't for her having to go above and beyond to regain Rednose's trust, she would've never let a loser like that get in her juice box.

"Baby, what's on your mind?" Rednose asked before he kissed her on the forehead. He noticed she had gotten quiet and was deep in meditation.

"Just was thinking about everything that happened last year. Plus, I still wanna go back to Columbus just to go visit my mother, brother, and other sister," Cee Money replied, sitting up and looking Rednose directly in the eyes.

This conversation had come up several times before, and each time, Rednose would dismiss the idea. "Baby, you know we can't go back right now. The city is still on fire. I'm not letting you out my presence. Them RRG members still got a few soldiers who probably still want some smoke. I'll never forgive myself if I let something happen to the mother of my only child. Don't worry because I still have some unfinished business we got to go handle soon. Just be patient, baby. Please bear with me a few more months. Let's just get to know our son. His little fat ass getting bigger too."

Rednose knew he couldn't stay secluded in his apartment located in Riverdale, Georgia. Although the area off Tara Boulevard was remote enough to keep a low profile, Rednose's mission was still incomplete. There were still some people he had to pay a visit to.

He had gotten sidetracked after the Carlos situation. Never would he underestimate anybody else again. That was a huge mistake. Rednose wasn't the type of person to lie to himself. He knew he had flaws, but he was a realist and could stand her straightening him out when he was wrong. He was dead wrong for letting emotions outweigh his wisdom. Although the hit on Carlos was a success, the after effect caused too many casualties. A reminder was indicated by his latest tattoo which read, "Long Live Ebony."

That was the one mistake that he had made. Carlos was him! Rednose underestimated his power and didn't take his retaliation team seriously until they made him. Those RRG members went hard about Carlos. They spun the block about this nigga all year. There were shootouts damn near every day. It wasn't even safe to go to the mall.

To make matters worse, there was another issue at hand —retaliation for Ice Water.

He was pretty sure some of the younger members who worshipped the ruthless young shooter wanted some revenge for Ice Water as well.

Honestly, he never planned to go to war immediately after his prison release. He did plan to transform into a samurai and slice down a list of people for different reasons he deemed as necessary. He made this list while he was still in prison. Only three of the people on the list were dead, and there were still more to go.

In the process, Rednose had made the city red hot upon his release last year. Now, he only squatted in the outskirts of Atlanta, Georgia if he wasn't in San Diego, California promoting his production company.

His company in San Diego was doing so well that they now had a podcast which streamed live twice a week. This brought in plenty of revenue from the internet. Rednose was also selling digital products online as well. He had mastered his craft by learning to make income off the dark web a long time ago.

His overall goal was to go legit via investing all his legal money in crypto currency. Rednose hoped to find someone who could help him come up with some ideas for investing wisely. With the rest of his money, he would invest in stocks and bonds. Rednose was very business savvy. Besides, Cee Money loved spending money, and she loved spending other people's money, including his. He'd already spent enough on the vacation to keep her mouth closed, but she still insisted that more money needed to be put up for their son, just in case of an emergency.

Cee Money regained his attention when she straddled him. She loved to jump on him early in the morning and ride him like crazy. She creamed on that dick so good that he put his hands behind his head and enjoyed every moment of it. This was how she got pregnant the first time. Having her feet flat on the queen-sized mattress and bouncing that fat ass up and down his dick always drove him crazy. So, before he came too fast inside her, he flipped her around and took her ass to pound town.

"Yass, yass! Ohhh, shit, Daddy, fuck this pussy. It's yours!" Cee Money was responding by shouting all those dirty words in his ear as he continued to thrust his hips up and down and side to side, digging deeper inside her pussy.

"You like that shit, don't you, girl?" Rednose knew she was in bliss by the look on her face.

"You the best, boo… Oh, my goodness! Fuck me!" Cee Money held her legs in the air and bit her bottom lip as she began to cum.

'Hell yeah, baby, cream on that dick... This pussy so hot and tight." Rednose wasn't exaggerating either. He loved fucking her. It never got boring. Cee Money was a super freak.

He had turned her out when he first got out of prison. She never had a guy stick his whole tongue inside her booty hole like Rednose did. He introduced her to bondage sex and made her fall in love with rough sex.

She remembered the first time he tied her up and gave her the wildest sex she'd ever experienced. He knew everything about her body. Just thinking about all the freaky things he'd been doing to her made her cum again back-to-back.

When Rednose was ready to cum, he spun her over on her stomach and started pounding her pussy like a dog in heat. She tried to escape by scrambling, but this only turned him on more. He always became aggressive whenever he was about to cum. He slapped her phat ass, causing it to jiggle, before he pulled out and shot a heavy load all over her backside.

"I love you, girl. Give me a kiss," Rednose spoke in a soft and gentle voice after he caught his breath.

"I love you too, you freak," Cee Money replied with a naughty grin plastered on her face.

Chapter 2

How did Coby survive a gunshot to the head with no brain damage? Not only did the bullet go through his head from point blank range, but the bullet also came out his eye. *But how?* thought Devin as he began to do research online. One website read...

"It's theoretically possible. There have been a handful of cases where people have been shot in the head and survived, but it's *remarkably* rare, and it almost always leads to drastic changes in either personality or cognitive ability.

"Bullets do lose energy as they go through the air due to friction. Point blank, the energy transfer from the bullet is an order of magnitude higher than one shot from a few hundred meters away. Also, point blank, the expanding gases and propellant from a gun is lethally devastating to the human head. It's how guns firing blanks are still able to kill people."

Coby was shot in the head, survived, and lost his eye in the process, Devin just didn't understand how. The most realistic scenario was that Rednose had to shoot him toward the top of the head, the bullet hitting the skull at a sharp enough angle to ricochet off and have the blunt force trauma of the point-blank shot take the eye out.

Coby had to remain in the intensive care unit (ICU) due to the massive internal bleeding to the brain from the impact of the bullet. Most of the bone around the top part of his skull and the eye would also be shattered to pieces by the gases. However, Coby was expected to make a full recovery. He was also expected to be kind of lame as he learned to walk and move around normally again. He would never be the same person.

It was amazing that he didn't have any brain damage. Devin figured that he came back just in time to save Coby's life. Luckily, the bullet went through his head and out of his eye. Although he lost the eye, it actually saved him from the lead poison and severe external bleeding and blood clots that would have caused brain damage. The bullet went inside the skull and outside the eye socket. It took several months, but Coby was back.

Devin had a plan, and he needed Coby at full strength in order to implement it. So, he decided to use all his resources to ensure that Coby made a full recovery. Today, Devin was going to introduce himself to Coby for the first time. The staff members at the hospital had told Devin that Coby would regain his consciousness today... It took Coby a while to get back healthy, but he made a full recovery. Well, it was not exactly a full recovery, but this was the best he was going to be. Devin looked at Coby, and fear instantly overcame him. With his eye missing, it gave Coby a scary new feature. He looked like a pirate gone mad.

"Who-who the fuck are you, and what-where t-the fuck am I?" Finally, Coby was waking up from a deep sleep. As he looked around the room, he did not recognize the environment. The lights were bright, and everything was white. He had recollection of nurses coming in and out, changing his IVs, but he did not recognize the dark-skinned young kid with the big afro sitting in the chair, staring at him. What stood out the most about the kid was a big ass afro that looked like he was ready to scream, "Black power."

"First of all, watch your mouth and calm down. You looking at the person that saved your life. My name is Devin, and we have a lot to discuss, but first, we got to get you all the way healthy, Coby." Devin stood up and stretched his arms behind his head as if he had been sitting in the chair for hours waiting on Coby.

Devin was only twenty years old, but he was a military baby and had a war mentality. His great-grandfather fought in World War II, and his father was a proud Marine. His mother died on duty in the Air Force. So, the way he was about to approach this revenge plot was strictly militant.

First of all, Coby had no idea who he was because they'd never met. Devin knew exactly who Coby was. Who didn't know the guy who went viral for shooting a video at the location that Carlos' body was removed from the tree? This was in Devin's favor because he planned to brainwash Coby and create false memories knowing that Coby's memory was completely damaged. Devin eavesdropped as the doctors discussed Coby's new mental condition. One of the side effects was that Coby now only had selective memory.

"How-how-how do you know my name, and what's wrong with my-my left eye?" Coby tried to remove the eye patch, but Devin stopped him.

"Woah, woah, woah. If I was you, I wouldn't do that, homie. Your eye was surgically removed because it was damaged beyond repair. If you make a full recovery, one day maybe you can get a new one." Devin tried to make light of the situation, knowing Coby would never find out the truth.

Devin went on to explain to Coby that he was involved in a major shootout. During the shootout, a lot of people were killed. As Devin described a little truth mixed in with a bunch of lies, he could see Coby's mind trying to register it, but he was totally lost. He had no idea what had really happened to him. He was absolutely clueless. Although the brain damage mostly came because of the gunshot, the drugs Coby was on at the time both hurt and helped him. The drugs had speed mixed in, and this ironically played a part in saving his life. This was the perfect setup for Devin to implement his plan.

He wanted to keep Coby addicted to the meth as he helped Coby get back strong through training and exercising. Once his body became dependent on the methamphetamine, he would continue to follow and listen to Devin like a loyal foot soldier. Devin read books and studied history a lot. He had read before that Adolf Hitler had his soldiers high on meth as they marched thirty days through the desert. When he was finished with Coby, he would be nothing more than a robot to him. This way, Devin could regroup and formulate a new team. This was Devin's opportunity to revamp RRG. When his soldiers became strong enough, that was when he would go after the guy responsible for killing Ice Water. Revenge on Rednose and Cee Money. Afterwards, he would personally finish off his new pawn, Coby, so Carlos could finally rest in peace. Devin was still under the impression that Coby was the one who hung Carlos.

Devin stared at Coby for a few minutes in complete disgust. He had lost so much weight and looked so weak. Ninety days of hard training and good eating would fix all that. Devin was a soldier, and he knew how to train a soldier.

"Why-why can't I-I see what's this on my eye?" Coby was trying to remove the eye patch again. Devin noticed that Coby was also stuttering as he spoke now. He guessed this had something to do with him being shot in the back of the head.

"Hey, nigga, chill! Damn, I just told you that your eye got removed. Don't touch it. Bro, you have to relax... Check this out though. I got something to show you." After Devin forced Coby to settle down, he got back to business.

"Look at this with your good eye," Devin said sarcastically and handed Coby an obituary.

The obituary had a beautiful picture of Ebony, and this did something to Coby instantly. For some reason, the machine began beeping loudly. The last time this happened, Devin asked the nurse why it did it. She simply explained it to him that the beeping noise in hospitals served multiple purposes, including alerting medical staff of changes in a patient's vital signs, reminding patients to take medication or perform certain tasks, and signaling the completion of medical equipment processes. It was also used as a communication tool between staff members with different beep patterns and tones indicating different messages. This constant background noise could be overwhelming for patients and visitors, but it was an essential part of the hospital's functioning and played a crucial role in patient care and safety.

However, this was not the case this time. Coby had instantly recognized the girl he knew as his sister for so long, Ebony. "It's okay, bro. I know who murdered her, and we are going to make him pay with his life."

Devin knew the medical team had been alerted of the beeping noises, so they were going to come in and make him leave. Just before they did, he took the obituary away and put it up. Next, he showed Coby a picture of Rednose and Cee Money. "He murdered your sister, Coby! He must die! You're not going to let your sister die in vain, are you?"

Before Coby could respond, a team of nurses and doctors were entering his room. "Excuse me, sir, we have to check on the patient now. Can you please step outside? Thanks."

Devin stepped outside and peeped through the small window. Once he was sure Coby was okay, he got on the elevator. Outside, he got inside his black van and rolled up the tinted window before making a quick phone call.

"Hello," the caller answered in a deep voice.

"It's time. Let's start the second half of this war. Halftime break is over. My duck is ready to be released. So, let's go snatch up the prey and hold him until I get Coby back to full strength. We going to wake the city back up with this act. They thought that wack ass tree hanging shit with Carlos went viral, wait until my next play get called!" Devin announced with rage. He was a crafty young cat and could become very dangerous because he had all the necessary resources.

The play Devin was going to call fresh out of halftime was going to restart this local war. He knew upon research and study that Rednose and Cee Money were no longer living in Columbus, Georgia or Phenix City, Alabama. Cee Money had moved out of her place in Phenix City shortly after the RRG members had invaded her home. Devin was there that night and remembered how deadly Rednose was with a pistol and a knife. So, he knew when it came to Rednose, his team would have to proceed with caution.

Furthermore, Cee Money was another issue. First of all, she was well connected and knew everything about RRG. She also had an older sister, Toria, who knew everything about RRG as well. Cee Money was the one that would actually buss her guns while Toria was good at seducing niggas for a setup.

Both of those females were really close to Carlos at one point in time. At one point in time, these were two of the baddest bitches in the city, and every big stepper affiliated with RRG would've paid to get inside either one of their fat pussies. They also had a brother who Devin was in the county jail with named Randy. Randy used to be a cool nigga, and they used to get money on the east side of town. Randy had made a name for himself on Forrest Road, one of the richest streets when it came to street money.

He lost all respect when he got addicted to the fentanyl. That was when the dogs, wolves, and hyenas began to attack him. He was already considered an out-of-town ass nigga. Those young boys on the east side were waiting for an excuse to take his money. Now, he was only an average street punk who stayed at a corner store with a bottle in his hand. He was the weak link.

There was also another sister who was still a minor, but what was weird was that she was nowhere on social media or anything. Devin didn't know her name or where she was.

No one had seen her since she was taken by Coby's team. He did remember that she was the sole reason the shootout transpired. Devin decided to just dismiss her as a nonthreat. Toria was hard to keep up with because she ran with different niggas every other week. She was outside real bad —_like outside the club and party house every time something was going on. The brother was so addicted to fentanyl that he was an easy target.

Devin was going to snatch up Randy and hold him hostage. It would be just like what happened to Carlos, except this time, it would be ten times worse!

"For every action there is an equal and opposite reaction! The halftime show is over. Payback time, pussies!" Devin chanted as he used a pick to style his afro.

Chapter 3

Cee Money tossed her hands in the air and started screaming in excitement when Rednose dropped the top on the Corvette that was painted a champagne color and sitting on new Forgiano wheels. They were on the highway en route to Miami where they were going to stay a few days before boarding the cruise ship. A seven-day cruise to the Bahamas was the vacation plan. It was a family vacation. In the backseat were Cee Money's baby sister and son.

Looking like fashion models, all four had just left the Marc Jacobs designer store. Cee Money had a designer green and white dress and a matching handbag. Rednose had a yellow Marc Jacobs designer shirt, a nice pair of designer jeans, and a pair of designer shades. Cee Money's baby sister, whose name was Keisha, was also looking nice in a pink Marc Jacobs designer skirt and turtleneck. Even Cee Money and Rednose's son was looking like a mini Rednose, wearing a matching outfit.

"Holiday Inn Port of Miami Downtown," Cee Money read the entrance sign when they pulled up. She used her freshly manicured green and white nails to move a few strands of hair from her eyes to get a full view of the beautiful setting. She looked so gorgeous that Rednose couldn't keep his hands off of her.

"'Important announcements: Pool is closed, and our airport shuttle has discontinued service. We apologize for the inconvenience.' What the fuck, brah?" cried Keisha, reading the sign that announced the pool was closed. All she had been saying the whole way to Miami was that she couldn't wait to go swimming.

The reason Rednose took her in and spoiled her with special attention was because of the things she went through. Although she was a young lady, she had a grown woman body. Rednose constantly had to stop grown men from trying to holler at her when they were in public. He figured bringing her on the seven-day cruise to the Bahamas would put a smile on her face. She had been through a lot since she was kidnapped. She still hadn't fully recovered yet. Since then, Rednose had been very overprotective about her. Also, it was easy to love her like a little sister because she reminded him of a younger Cee Money.

"Awwwww, Keisha, don't worry, little sister. When we get to the Bahamas, I promise we're gonna have so much fun that you're not going to be worried about anythingg," said Rednose, stroking her cheeks like she was a little baby. In response, she started blushing and cheered up instantly.

"Big ass baby!" said Cee Money, rolling her eyes at Keisha in the rearview mirror before getting out of the car. She was such a hater. She wanted all the attention from Rednose but was happy he treated her little sister like his own.

Keisha was in love with her nephew. She thought that was her little baby. Although "Little Rednose" was almost two years old and could talk, she treated him like an infant.

After valet parking, the family of four observed the beautiful sight. Cee Money strolled online and read more information about the hotel. "Okay, y'all, listen up... This is what we paying for." Cee Money began to read out loud what she read online.

"Enjoy your stay near the Port of Miami. The Holiday Inn Port of Miami-Downtown is the perfect place to stay for your next trip to Miami. Located just six minutes from the Port of Miami, our hotel is close to all the major attractions in the city. Within walking distance of our hotel, you'll find Bayside Marketplace, the Kaseya Center, and the American Airlines Arena. Bayside Marketplace is a must-visit for any shopper with over one hundred fifty stores and restaurants. The Kaseya Center is a hub for technology and innovation, and the American Airlines Arena is home to the Miami Heat basketball team. The Metromover station behind our hotel makes it easy to get around Downtown Miami and Brickell. The Metromover is a free elevated train that connects major points of interest in the area. After a long day of exploring, return to our hotel to relax in our modern accommodations. Our rooms are spacious and comfortable with free Wi-Fi, blackout shades, HDTVs with streaming capabilities, and a mini fridge. We offer specials and packages designed to make your stay even more enjoyable, and we have a variety of onsite amenities.

"Downtown Miami is a vibrant and exciting place to be, and it's known for hosting a variety of special events throughout the year. Some of the most popular events include the ING and Mercedes-Benz Marathon, Market America, Miami Film Festival and Book Fair, Art Basel, and Ultra Music Fest. Whatever brings you to Miami, enjoy your stay at The Holiday Inn Port of Miami-Downtown."

The next few days were an absolute blast. They spent so much money, purchased so many souvenirs, and had so much fun. They almost lost track of time and nearly forgot the next morning was the first day of the seven-day cruise to the Bahamas. They decided to stay in the last night and get some rest, so they could be fully energized when they boarded the cruise.

The next morning after eating a full breakfast, the family of four checked out of the hotel and loaded up all their luggage and expensive souvenirs. Rednose gassed up and hit the road, headed toward the seaport.

"Get ready for fun in the sun when you cruise to The Bahamas from Miami for seven days aboard our award-winning cruise ships, including the extensively renovated Norwegian Sky. Only Norwegian gives you more choices of what to do and see on your vacation with the freedom and flexibility of Freestyle Cruising. Whether you are looking for the perfect Labor Day Cruise or a reason to escape for the weekend, your possibilities are as open as the sea. Dress up or down. Swim with dolphins. Sip on coconuts. The perfect weekend vacation awaits." Keisha's voice was full of excitement as she read the brochure.

"Yay, I get to swim with dolphins! Oh, my God!" she boasted like an innocent child. Her childish nature made Rednose's heart melt and tickled Cee Money deep in her belly.

Rednose had a friend named Tiffany that he went to high school with, and now, she was a travel agent. This was very beneficial because he was able to get a good location for his family on the cruise ship. It was worth every penny. For each day, there was a different activity to indulge in.

Everything was going well the first couple days. There was no stress or worries, only positive energy and positive minds. The sky was so beautiful, and the sun lit the water up, giving it a bluish green color. Dolphins were jumping in and out of the ocean. It was so amazing to see.

The food was so delicious. Never before in his life had Rednose had an octopus and vegetable dinner. The cook said that if he liked it then he should try squid because it tasted just like octopus. Cee Money's ratchet, ghetto ass was in love with the fried shark. Her country ass kept talking about it tasting exactly like chicken. Keisha kept it simple with some fried shrimp and crab legs which she also fed Little Rednose.

The next day was when things started to get a little weird. First of all, Keisha and Little Rednose got lost some kind of way.

"What the fuck you mean you can't find my son and my fucking sister? Nigga, are you crazy?" Cee Money began to panic, screaming at Rednose all loud in front of everybody after hours of no contact from Keisha. To make matters worse, her iPhone kept going straight to voicemail. This made Cee Money panic even more.

At first, Rednose tried to remain calm under pressure. He notified the security, but after another hour went by, he began to get nervous as well.

"This cannot be happening again. I know my sister did not get kidnapped again! WHERE is my son? Oh, my God!" Cee Money was panicking, which caused Rednose's anxiety level to rise.

All of a sudden, the security guard grabbed Rednose and pointed in the direction where he noticed Keisha and his son sitting next to some Jamaican old lady, playing some type of card game. This was a relief because his son looked so peaceful. However, the old lady sitting across from Keisha and his son instantly gave Rednose a bad vibe before he even walked up to them.

"Keisha, bitch, I'm going to kill you! DON'T you ever fucking disappear like that again! Do you understand me? Let's go right now!" yelled Cee Money as she snatched her sister up. She didn't care she was embarrassing herself in front of everybody. Rednose grabbed his son, who wrapped his arms around his father and kissed his face. He loved his dad so much.

"Let me read your horoscope, rude boy?" the funny looking Jamaican lady asked Rednose, shocking everybody as she shuffled a deck of Tarot cards.

"No, hell nawl. I don't play with black magic! You the devil. Stay away from my family! I don't wanna see you again while I'm on this ship!" Rednose declared with authority.

"You can't run from the past. Crush your enemies totally or they will come back and hunt you forever! Sometimes, you are behind enemy lines, and sometimes, you sleep with the enemy... Enjoy your cruise, rude boy." The old Jamaican lady did a wicked laugh and counted some cards until she got the number seven and flipped over a card of death. She looked at it for a while and then got her things and disappeared into the crowd of party girls.

Rednose advised security about the old lady, but security said he didn't see her or know anything about what he was talking about. Rednose and his family went back to their room very uncomfortably. The last few days weren't even fun anymore. Cee Money was ready to go. She didn't let Keisha or her son out of her eyesight until they were off the ship.

Even after they got back to Miami and even on the highway back to Georgia, Rednose kept thinking about the old Jamaican lady and her cold statement.

"You can't run from the past. Crush your enemies totally or they will come back and hunt you forever! Sometimes, you are behind enemy lines, and sometimes, you sleep with the enemy... Enjoy your cruise, rude boy."

She'd flipped over the seventh cards in the deck, and it was the death card. Rednose wasn't naive about Tarot cards. He knew that the ancient civilizations a long time ago used to believe in horoscopes and spiritual realms. The death card meant the end of something or the beginning of something new, or sometimes, it meant literal death. Rednose was a very spiritual person, and he was accepted by his ancestors. However, he also believed in evil spirits and knew he had a lot of demons chasing after his soul. For some reason, her words kept replying over and over again in his head all the way back to Riverdale.

"You can't run from the past. Crush your enemies totally or they will come back and hunt you forever! Sometimes, you are behind enemy lines, and sometimes, you sleep with the enemy... Enjoy your cruise, rude boy."

As soon as they got back on Tara Boulevard, Cee Money's phone began ringing constantly. When she answered the phone, Rednose could hear her mother screaming and yelling something about how they needed to come home because her brother, Randy, was missing, and nobody had seen or heard from him. Cee Money told her mother she didn't have time for the bullshit because she'd had a long weekend.

Rednose didn't think the phone call was a big deal until it started ringing again. This time, it was the older sister, Toria. She announced that word on the street was that her brother, Randy, had gotten snatched up and was being held for ransom. Toria was telling Cee Money that the word on the street was that niggas were looking for her, and she needed to pop out. Nobody had heard from or seen Randy in over a week.

Upon hearing this, Rednose started to put two and two together and knew that halftime was over, and the second half of the war was about to crank up. He knew it wasn't over but didn't expect things to escalate this fast.

He knew that he would have to pay a visit back to the city of death real soon.

"You can't run from the past. Crush your enemies totally or they will come back and hunt you forever! Sometimes, you are behind enemy lines, and sometimes, you sleep with the enemy... Enjoy your cruise, rude boy." The old Jamaican lady's words replayed over and over in his head. Cee Money and Rednose locked eyes with no words.

Chapter 4

Ryan was living his best life in San Diego, California. He was the man out there! Ryan was only twenty-seven years old and was very ambitious. Although he was a full-blooded white man dripping in pop culture, he had a Black boy swag as well.

This was one of the main reasons Rednose decided to let him run his entertainment business. He could cross over between two different cultural groups. For example, with Ryan being tall, well built, and handsome, he could mingle with the white people and could fit right in with the Black people because of his hood swag. Not only that, but he was also a wild card because he had Dominican and Puerto Rican connections.

Resembling a tall, athletic Justin Bieber, Ryan thrived to be a movie star so badly, and he was damn near famous already. When him and Rednose first decided to do business, Rednose made it clear that he didn't want anything to do with the fame. The short screenplays were fashioned by Rednose, and Ryan was destined to star in his role.

Back in the day, Rednose used to be one of the assistant coaches for the baseball team that Ryan used to play for, that was how they first met when they were younger. They were cool before Rednose even jumped off the porch. Before he went to prison, they created plans of getting inside the entertainment world.

After moving to the West Coast, Ryan took the industry by storm. He made all the right connections within the film industry. In just two years, Ryan had made more connections than solo actors who'd been trying to get a gig for the past decade. The podcast was getting bigger and bigger each week. And now, it had at least a million streamers that tuned in.

What Rednose didn't know was that Ryan had developed a new habit. He'd began playing with his nose, and he liked to have hardcore sex while he was geeked up on drugs. Ryan didn't think there was a problem. That was why he didn't tell Rednose. He felt like he could handle his habit because he could still function. Today, he was having some fun with two snow bunnies that he met when he went to the zoo.

One's name was Stacy, and the other's name was Brittany. Stacy was a redhead who was short and thick and sexy everywhere. Brittany was a typical blonde with some nice titties and a lot of curves. Ryan had a bowl of coke, and all three were high as hell right now. They'd been having great sex for the past forty-five minutes. Ryan was a big freak being the Scorpio that he was.

"Yes, yes, yes, yes, yes, Ryan! Give it to me!" shouted Stacy as she let Ryan have his way with her.

Brittany was so geeked up that she an in a trance. She was just lying on the bed, watching Ryan and Stacy fuck like wild animals.

Stacy was on all fours, letting Ryan enjoy the artwork displayed all over her backside. Ryan put a pair of handcuffs on Brittany and made Stacy eat her cat while he continued to pound her hot wet pussy. Her kitty got so wet when she was high on coke.

Brittany would do anything, so Ryan was used to slutting her out, but Stacy was a hard one to crack, so this was very sensational for the stud, Ryan, to be jumping up and down in her guts.

All of a sudden, the front door opened, and a tall, model looking, video vixen stepped in wearing four-inch heels and crashed the party.

"Son of a bitch, you fucking moron! What the hell do you think you're doing here?" Melissa went insane as she began to throw wild punches on both females at the same time.

Melissa was a beautiful, sandy brown head type with almond eyes and beautiful skin. This was Ryan's fiancée, and this was not the first time she had caught Ryan having an affair on her. As usual, she would whoop the girls' ass, and they would get the hell out of there. Then, she would turn her fury on Ryan. He would just sit there and take all the punches until she calmed down and began to cry and call him an "asshole."

"It's not what you think, babe... I'm just having fun. They don't mean shit to me. Damn it!" Ryan's face was red, and his nose was running.

"Oh, my God, are you high?" Melissa asked, noticing the residue on his nose. "I thought you stopped doing that shit? It's fine... Okay, that's it. I'm calling your boss. I'm going to tell Rednose! He needs to make a trip down here! You're getting out of hand now. You wasn't like this at first. This shit is becoming ridiculous." Melissa rolled her eyes and stormed away, making her four-inch heels click clack with each step as she whipped out her iPhone and proceeded to dial Rednose's number.

"No, don't call him!! Hey, don't you put my fucking personal business out there like that... Are you out of your damn mind? Huh, what the fuck? GIVE me the fucking phone." Ryan was ashamed and embarrassed as he rushed behind Melissa and snatched her phone out of her hand.

"Give me my fucking phone! Goddamn it!" Melissa complained as she began to wrestle with Ryan for her phone.

Melissa wasn't weak; she was actually strong for a female, but Ryan was way stronger than her. After a few minutes of struggle, he had the phone in his hand, and he slapped the shit out of her, and she fell on the bed.

"Now, listen here. Let me explain something to you, you little spoiled bitch... Don't you never ever in your fucking life get in my personal business and threaten to call my motherfucking boss on me! I'm in charge! Do you understand me, whore? I can do what the fuck I motherfucking want to do! I'm the man in San Diego! I run shit around here. You better ask some damn body. Not Rednose, but me. I'm the man. We are both the boss! The fuck you mean call my boss? Are you nuts? Now get your shit and get the fuck out my apartment, you fucking slut!" Ryan's adrenaline was rushing. The cocaine was good. He didn't realize he was wigging out.

Melissa wiped the tears off her face while staring darts at Ryan. She gathered her few things to leave without another word.

Ryan watched her slam the door and instantly regretted how he'd just disrespected the woman of his dreams. He knew his coke habit was getting out of hand. At first, it was just for recreational use. It started off when he moved to San Diego and experienced the night life.

From promoting to advertising, he began to go to all the entertainment parties. He would be in the nightclubs and inside the VIP sections with all the divas and video vixens. He was just using a little to be amped up and stay up all night because he had to work on editing all the videos and production.

Now, he was using it out of habit. This wasn't fun anymore. He was messing up his best relationship now. He knew he had to do something and real soon before it was too late.

Interrupting his thought process, he heard some movement outside the front door and knew it was Melissa coming back to get her iPhone. He cheered up and walked toward the front and was about to open the door with open arms. Ryan wanted to apologize, but as soon as he opened the door, Melissa stood upright, breasts up high, with a stare on her face he'd never seen before, carrying a loaded small handgun. She forced her way back inside while aiming directly at his chest.

"Now it's your turn to listen, you bastard! I'm sick of your shit, Ryan... I should shoot you in your got damn face. Give me one fucking reason why not?" Melissa now had tears coming down her face. When the woman was fed up, boy, you better run or start talking, and I mean fast.

***

Nya was trying to figure out why her ex-boyfriend, Tyler, was so obsessed with her. The more she tried to pull away from him, the more he would pursue her. He wasn't stalking her or anything, but he was becoming very aggressive and didn't understand that she needed some space.

Her baby face and caramel complexion made it hard for any guy to take his eyes off of her. Yes, she was kind of skinny but had a nice little frame. She was what you called slim-thick. She had long, black hair and a grown woman body that was very curvy. Not only that, even when she was on her professional style, her beauty was breathtaking. Also, she was very flexible.

The guy that she always thought about was the guy she met a while ago at a nightclub.

It was Rednose, but he was across the country. They talked from time to time, but she wanted to get more attention.

Her whole life, it had been the opposite. All guys went to the extreme to get her attention. She wasn't used to this reverse role. Rednose barely called her. The only time they talked was when she would reach out. Nya was spoiled and was used to getting what she wanted by any means necessary.

After they met at the club, she became cool with Ryan and decided to help him promote the podcast just to get close to Rednose. She knew he was coming to the West Coast in a few weeks, and she couldn't wait. She just had to avoid her crazy ex-boyfriend, Tyler.

Nya was the head coach of the University of San Diego dance team. She started dancing at the age of seven and was competing nationally in jazz, hip hop, acrobatics, and lyrical at age eleven. She won numerous awards throughout her youth and high school dance career.

Furthermore, Nya was a University of San Diego alumni and used to dance for the University of San Diego dance team, which consistently placed in the top five of the Hip-Hop Division 1 category at USA Collegiate Dance Nationals. After graduating from the University of San Diego, Nya stepped into the pro cheer and dance world as a San Diego Charger girl. She had worked with many esteemed choreographers. Nya was famous all over San Diego, California because she continued to work with young dancers in the high school.

She was also involved with advocating for missing young girls in the area. In the last two years, five young females had come up missing in the San Diego area. Nya donated a lot of money to the foundations dedicated to protecting the young women in the area. Unfortunately, she couldn't protect herself from her boyfriend, Tyler. Maybe when Rednose came to visit, she could convince him to stay. After seeing her with a new man, maybe Tyler would move on — or maybe not.

Her thought process was interrupted when her phone started going off with notifications. Some members of the production team called her to notify her that the live stream podcast was going to be cancelled this week because Ryan had been rushed to the emergency room.

"Oh, my goodness, excuse me, ladies. I have an emergency... Ummm, I have to leave," Nya announced, rushing to get inside of her red BMW.

She had just received news that Ryan had been shot twice and was in critical condition. The sad part was she wasn't even thinking about Ryan's well-being. She was looking for an opportunity to get close to Rednose. She knew he would hop on the next plane about his best friend, Ryan.

This was her chance to make her move on the man she had a crush on. She knew she had to find a way to get him alone, so she could make her offer to him. She just hoped he was the man she thought he could be for the job. She hoped he would not think she was crazy or exposed her operation. If he did, things would end badly for him. If he played his cards right, she would make him a millionaire.

Chapter 5

The last thing Randy remembered was being snatched up aggressively and thrown into the back of a van. Now, he was bound in some type of cage with a mouth guard and duct tape around his mouth. He was on his knees with his hands tied behind his back. Also, his feet were chained together. He could hear a few guys talking but couldn't see anything.

What put the fear in him was all the loud noise around him that kept echoing. It sounded like metal slapping against steel. Each sound got louder and louder. He had to be in some type of warehouse or an open building because of all the echoing. He could smell fresh paint. This must've been some type of workshop. He tried his best to break loose and get free. He had no idea why he was being held hostage.

Although he had a bad drug habit and was a slave of the fentanyl, he didn't owe anybody. He really didn't do bad business because, although he went broke, his family still had money, and he had a baby mama that had a good ass job and would do anything for him although she was bad looking bad. Although a retired prostitute, she loved Randy with all of her heart, so she never had any problem supporting his habit. *So, why am I being treated so maliciously?* he wondered.

He remembered seeing a dark-skinned, husky guy with a huge afro, looking like some type of military comeback officer, approach him before he was snatched up and forced in the van. When he tried to resist, the dark-skinned guy with the huge afro threw him into a chokehold so swiftly that he was sleep in no time. It was something about the husky, dark skinned guy with the huge afro that made him very nervous. The wicked spirit called Randy's name, and at that point, he knew that he was in danger.

All of a sudden, the bandana that was over his face was removed. It was as if the veil of a new realm had been opened, as if the gates of hell had been opened. Randy could not believe his eyes. It took a few moments for his eyes to adjust to the brightness, but surely after that, he noticed all the strange objects and knew he was about to be tortured.

Directly in front of him stood the husky, dark-skinned guy with a huge afro. He was holding a metal bat wrapped in barbed wire. He was surrounded by four other guys that had on ski masks. All five guys had matching army fatigue outfits and army boots on. Nobody said anything. They were all just staring at Randy. Randy responded by not saying anything as well. He didn't know what to say or what to do. Randy squeezed his eyes when he noticed something behind the guys.

It only took a few moments to realize what it was. It was a huge blow torch made of metal. All of a sudden, the husky, dark-skinned guy with a huge afro swung the bat directly over his head, but he missed, hitting him on purpose. Next, he burst out into a wicked, loud laugh. He was spooky.

"Randy, Randy, Randy... did I spook you, bro? I'm not going to hit you with this metal bat. Nah, I'm not that type of person, but I do have one question. I'm going to ask you, and if you don't respond the way I wish, you will regret it instantly. Do you understand me? Do I make myself clear?" Devin's voice was heavy and loud. He was in combat mode.

"Okay," Randy quickly replied.

"Say yes sir!" Devin ordered.

"Huh?" Randy was puzzled.

"I said say yes sir right now!" Devin flexed at Randy as he barked his order once more.

"YES, SIR!" Randy repeated, sounding like a nigga bitch.

"Okay, now the question is... Where is Cee Money?"

"Who? My sister, Ciara?" Randy quizzed, looking stupid.

"Wrong answer, nigga! Now, I just told you if you don't respond the way I wish, you would regret it instantly." Devin cleared his throat and looked to his left hand.

Standing directly next to him was someone Randy knew for sure was dead. He could not believe his eyes. The notorious Coby took off his ski mask, revealing a hideous appearance that sent chills throughout Randy's entire body.

He looked like something off a horror film. First of all, you could tell he had been shot in the head because of all the scalp wounds. The stitches and staples left ugly, damaged tissue all over his head. Furthermore, he wasn't wearing an eye patch or glass eye for that matter. This gave him an evil look. The ugly motherfucker had an eye missing.

This had to be impossible. Randy was looking at a dead man. Coby was dead, according to the streets. How could he survive a head shot from point blank range? Impossible! *Ugly as he is, he would of been better off dead*, Randy thought to himself.

Before Randy had any time to question the unreal reality, Coby took the metal bat wrapped in barbed wire out of Devin's hands and slapped it across Randy's face. Randy was a heavy-set, bright skinned guy, so his body fell back with a loud bang, and his face became discolored almost instantly. The impact even made Devin frown up. Randy was unconscious.

***

Cee Money's mother, Trina, and her sister, Toria, were cooking up a storm —_barbeque chicken breasts, potato salad, cheesy squash, macaroni and cheese, spinach, carrots, deviled eggs, collard greens with neck bones, butter beans with ham hocks, and cornbread made like pancakes. Those girls were going hard in the kitchen. Everything was all good before somebody rang the doorbell, and that was when all hell broke loose.

"Baby, answer the door. I'm about to pull out the macaroni from the oven. Everything else almost ready!" Ms. Trina yelled with her big booty in the air.

She was bending over to reach inside the oven. She looked like an older version of Cee Money with way more hips and ass. She had ghetto tattoos and piercings everywhere like your typical hoodrat. She was a country girl at heart from Albany, Georgia, a seasoned whore who had passed the game to her ratchet ass daughters. Guys didn't have any wins against these sexy, sneaky, money hungry bitches. They played a lot of stupid games which would eventually lead to stupid prices.

Toria was the oldest daughter and had all of her mom's ass on her. She wasn't as pretty as Cee Money, but she was still fine as hell. What made up for her lack of beauty was that she could suck the shit out of a dick and loved to twerk her big phat ass everywhere she'd go and all over the internet. She was a straight up slut hoe. She got a lot of attention because of how nasty and freaky she was. You had to be careful though because she was trifling and would do anything for money.

In her twenty-seven years alive, she had become a professional scam artist and trick hoe. She helped set up so many niggas, masquerading as a Black, innocent queen that you would have thought she knew how to play chess. Karma was so real that nobody saw it coming until it knocked at their front door.

Not too long ago, she had already got herself into a dangerous situation because of the type of ruthless, rough guys she and her partner-in-crime, Cee Money, were involved with. Yet she still could not leave the ghetto ass street life alone.

"Okay, Mama, you know your company on the way. You need to put some damn clothes on. Them men already get to touching and feeling on people when y'all be drinking." Toria rolled her eyes and proceeded to see who was at the front door.

When Toria opened the front door, nobody was there. She was about to close the door when she saw a big ass, old school looking, black van pull up in front of her house. She didn't think anything of it. She heard someone pop the latches and let the door slide. The next thing she saw almost made her heart stop beating.

Two guys wearing army fatigue and black ski masks were carrying her brother, Randy, like he was a baby. Randy was not a small person, so they scared the shit out of her. Next, before she could say anything, they were pouring gasoline on her brother, then they set him on fire. One of them had a big ass afro, and he looked very dangerous. He had some type of blow torch in his hand, and when he squeezed it, the flames grew bigger on Randy.

"Agggggghhhh! Agggggghhhh! Help me!" Randy cried, running toward the front door with the top half of his body in flames.

Toria was in shock. She was speechless and could not move. She never experienced anything like this, and she was going to be traumatize forever —_if she survived.

It looked like something you would see in a horror movie. It looked like something you'd only see on TV. These niggas just pulled up and tossed her brother in the front yard and set him on fire in front of her. It was around 5 p.m. —_broad daylight. It was in the middle of the day. What made matters worse was that her mother's house was on the main street. Some of the kids who had gotten out of school a few hours ago were outside. Some parents who had been working all day were just coming home. A lot of the neighbors were starting to come outside.

"Toria, who out here screaming like they crazy?! Oh, my God! What the fuck?! My baby burning alive!" Trina ran to the side of the house, searching for the water hose.

While all the commotion was going on, Coby, Devin, and the rest of the guys pulled out assault rifles and Dracos then began to shoot the house up while Randy's body was still burning. Devin wasn't playing when he said he was about to take this shit viral, way worse than the last time. Yes, he ran away during the main shootout that ended his uncle, Ice Water's, life. However, he had spun back around the block to begin part two of this war. Halftime was over, and Devin was making it known publicly. This nigga was crazy with his big ass afro flying in the air as he shot the Draco, aiming at Randy. He knew he was about to go viral.

The last viral incident in the city was when Rednose killed Carlos on Instagram Live. Coby had claimed responsibility for it, but Devin knew the truth. Now, he was doing a copycat stunt. Devin's performance was planned out perfectly. He was a military baby. He stayed near the van because he had somebody inside recording the entire incident.

They let over one hundred rounds go. Randy was shot dead before they could put the fire out. He fell down on the grass, still burning, with over forty holes in his body. Toria got hit a few times as well. Trina was fast enough to drop to the ground and roll under her vehicle that was parked in her driveway. Unfortunately, she couldn't save Randy, but she was more concerned about her safety.

After a few minutes of shooting, the van sped away. Devin just sat in the back of the van again, his afro back into a nice style with a sick look on his face. He took the cell phone out of the person's hand, who was recording, and made sure all the action was caught on camera. Now, all he had to do was post this shit on the internet just like Rednose had done when they jammed on Carlos. Payback time was now.

Coby had no idea he was working for the enemy. His brain was not fully healed, and he was kind of slow now. Devin had portrayed as a friend who could help him get back healthy, which he did for ninety days. He promised him that he would help find the killer who killed Ebony. He had brainwashed Coby into thinking Rednose was the one that killed Ebony. Devin was the new face of RRG.

"This shit going to be on CNN," he said out loud to no one in particular, now picking his big afro.

Devin was a menace.

Chapter 6

"Those maniacs killed my baby! Good Lawd! Those bastards are heartless! They rode up and parked in front of my house and threw my baby out of a black van! They used a metal looking blow torch and set my son on fire! He didn't deserve this hideous act!" Trina and over five hundred members of the community were rallying with protesters downtown by the government center.

The city was outraged, and they were not about to respond peacefully. The city was outside today. Among the group of people protesting were a few preachers, lawyers, off duty cops, and even police officers. However, most of the crowd was a bunch of angry Black sisters.

Trina was so heartbroken as she welcomed the condolences. They mourned the death of Randy. His death hit different because not only was he burned severely, but he was shot over forty times. He would definitely be having a closed casket funeral, or he could be cremated.

Maybe it would be best to cremate the rest of his remains. Honestly, no family could bear to see anybody sitting inside a casket looking like that. This family was cursed.

Everybody was sending love and prayers for the speedy recovery of Toria. A few stray bullets hit her in nonlife threatening areas. She would be in the hospital until further notice.

This was like deja vu for the city of Columbus, Georgia. It had been less than two years since the most vicious crime took place. The incident had gone viral with a guy hanging from a tree while the wood cabin near the tree was burning. This had triggered a crime spree and bloody war.

This was the copycat response! It was happening all over again. Devin had set it up for the camera phone to capture it all. He had studied and copied the same type of strategy Rednose once implemented when he first got out of prison and was moving like a reckless barbarian and was on the mental health crazy shit. Devin knew what type of reaction he would get, and that was exactly why he recorded the entire incident and had it put on the internet via the dark web.

After it was released, everybody was very emotional. The entire city was upset. Something had to be done immediately!

"This community is not safe! Get these gang banging bastards off the streets! They shot my house up while my son was burning alive! They killed my dog too! My daughter was shot by them sons of bitches! My daughter is gonna be okay. She just needs some time. to heal They used assault rifles to shoot up my house, knocking off wood chunks! They shattered my windows, and I did not have any insurance on my property. I don't know how I'm going to pay to get everything fixed! They killed my baby. Y'all got to do something. This community is not safe. I'm sick and tired of the virus... When is it going to stop?!" Trina was crying and screaming.

She had real tears in her eyes and snot falling all over her face. This woman had the crowd in an uproar now. They got crazy and then became very aggressive for the police on security.

All of a sudden, a few other protesters began to bumrush the officers out of rage and anger. A fight broke out between two females, and that started more fights. Now it was a big brawl in the middle of the street. Nobody noticed the black van ducked off in a secluded area, watching everything that took place. Inside the van, Devin was picking his big afro, watching all the action.

"See, I told y'all niggas... We got the streets going crazy. Real right guys, we back in this motherfucker. Just be patient. Cee Money and Rednose will pop back in the city real soon. I do this shit for Ice Water. I do this shit for Carlos," Devin chanted to himself, making sure Coby wasn't paying attention, while still picking his big afro in a neat style.

After making one of his soldiers record some of the fighting at the protest, Devin pulled off in the black van. The reason he was still recording the aftermath of his damage was because he was going to let Coby shoot a new video. Just like he did with the clout he gained from Carlos' death, Coby was going to get famous off of Randy's death.

Not only did Devin put Coby on his hardcore workout plan and nutritious diet to prepare his body for war, but he had also been feeding Coby drugs. He had brainwashed Coby. He made him submit and follow all his commands to the point that if he didn't do what Devin said, Coby could not get high.

"We will use all that footage... Hell yeah, you're going to be the man, bro. This is your moment. After the city see this, it will make you famous again, Coby. Do you understand me, huh?" Devin was boasting Coby's self-esteem up.

"I'm the man!" Coby replied, looking at the footage of the protest with his only eye.

Devin laughed at Coby's retarded body movement. It was absolutely insane. Devin turned up his music and zoned out. Now that halftime was over, he had to prepare for the counterpunch.

His research revealed that Cee Money had a lot of resources. He didn't know much about her baby daddy, Rednose, so he didn't fear him much, which was going to be a big mistake. Although he was proclaiming that RRG was back and stronger than ever, he knew that wasn't true.

Coby had a few loyal soldiers that didn't even know he was alive yet. So, if Devin wanted to get his numbers up, he had to make Coby the man and become a wolf wearing sheep clothing. He was going to impersonate as a sidekick, playing the role of being the second option, although he was really the first in command. No one had to know the truth until it was time. A force that could not be seen could not be shut down.

Once Coby's new video dropped, his small army of flunkies would come running to ride Coby's wave. By using Coby's soldiers along with his own, Devin's numbers would increase. Then, he would be comfortable enough to attack Cee Money and Rednose with an ambush they'd never see coming.

***

Things were so intense between Rednose and Cee Money. It had been a few days since the clip of Randy's gruesome murder went viral, followed by the violent protest. Cee Money had been on some bipolar shit ever since she found out her brother was killed, and her sister was in the hospital.

She had totally flipped the script out of the blue on Rednose. She was acting like a different person out of nowhere. The good news was that Rednose was expecting this. Clever is as clever does. He was already two steps ahead of her.

He knew what type of person he was dealing with. He knew she was playing a role because of his resources and because she was afraid of him retaliating against her for crossing him in the beginning. He knew it was only a matter of time before she revealed her true hand.

Unlike her, he never let his poker face disappear. He was just playing her very close. He didn't question her strange behavior yet; he just let her vent. Her baby sister, Keisha, was the one he felt bad for.

She hadn't stopped crying since the tragic incident. All of her friends in high school had seen the disgusting video on the internet. Everyone was calling her, sending their condolences. In fact, she was the first to see the video. Her initial reaction was so dramatic. She ran in the room while Cee Money was bouncing her big, round booty up and down on Rednose's hardness. They were in the middle of having hardcore sex when, all of a sudden, Keisha rushed in like a running back with a video of a man on fire.

Rednose went limp instantly. The shit scared the hell out of him. It was like he was having deja vu all over again... or was this karma? Was this karma being born right before his eyes? Right at his front door for the things he'd done shortly after his release from a ten-year prison bid a few years ago?

Cee Money sure as hell felt like it was all his fault. If looks could kill, Rednose would have been dead a thousand times. Cee Money felt like she was dealing with a psychopath that caused things to become negative in her life. Before she met Rednose, she had never been through anything like she had in the last few years.

She never knew one man could cause so much evil. One bad seed had destroyed her whole family. First, Carlos, then her older sister got kidnapped, then her baby sister got kidnapped. Now, her mother's house had been shot up, and her brother was killed —all because of something Rednose did while he was in his feelings.

If Rednose would have listened to her and let the situation with Carlos go, none of this shit would have ever happened. Although she hadn't gotten all the exclusive details, she made a few phone calls. Word on the street was that those RRG members were back for retaliation for the death of not only Carlos but Ice Water as well.

Due to these circumstances, she was stuck between a rock and a hard place. For one, she couldn't just pop back up because they were surely to seek justice on her. She had to move swiftly if she wanted to remain ahead of the circle of death. There was no way Cee Money would let her family's tragic event lure her into a trap. There was no way she would go out like that. She was too advanced for her own good. Cee Money was all for herself. Yes, she loved her family, but she loved herself more. Nobody came to rescue her when she was getting molested by her perverted ass family member! Where the fuck was Randy at then? She was a cold shoulder individual anyway by nature, but she played it off by acting like she gave a fuck about life.

Cee Money was the smartest out of the bunch. That was why she got back with Rednose —_because she needed security and protection. She knew she could not make it on her own after all the war zone aftermath. Soon as she saw her brother's body burning alive, the words of the old Jamaican lady on that cruise began playing in her head over and over again like a song on repeat.

"You can't run from the past. Crush your enemies totally or they will come back and hunt you forever! Sometimes, you are behind enemy lines, and sometimes, you sleep with the enemy... Enjoy your cruise, rude boy."

Mr. Clever himself felt the energy from two planets away. Rednose didn't need to hear her speak a word out loud. He could read her mind because he was tapped in spiritually. He had high priest and ancestors who protected him no matter what he did. Therefore, he knew what she was thinking.

Cee Money knew her baby daddy very well because every man spilled his heart out to the woman he loved. What she didn't know was that Rednose was dealing with his own insecurity and anxiety. Was all this his fault? Could he have been smarter when he first got out and avoided all this nonsense? Either way, he didn't regret anything because the past was the past, and now, it was time. He had to deal with what was in front of him.

No matter what happened in the past, he wasn't going out bad at all. Plus, he wasn't going to sit back and wait on karma to get him. He was up on the score. Nobody wanted the smoke with him because he was the chosen one. He was raised by a real warrior.

Rednose always said that he chased his fears. For example, while it could snow in the desert, it was unusual. He'd stated that if he saw a five-hundred-pound lion stalking him, he would chase it! He was going to meet it halfway. That was why he had gone ahead and made a secret trip to the storage area and pulled out all of his weapons and snuck them in the duffle bag. Mentally, he wasn't prepared for a trip back to the city of death.

Cee Money's mother was upset with her because she hadn't shown her face yet.

Trina felt like Cee Money was being disrespectful toward the family because her brother was dead, and her sister was in the hospital, yet she was still out of town.

Keisha was also homesick and ready to go back to Columbus to visit her family and see her friends. Nobody had seen her since she had been abducted by Coby last year. Fortunately, she was rescued by Cee Money and Rednose. A lot of time had passed since then, but the poor baby was still very shaken up by that incident. Rednose had been playing the hero and protector. She enjoyed hiding in comfort under his wing, but now, it was time for all three of them to pop back out.

Cee Money was acting really funny, and Rednose was tired of her shit. She kept making these weird phone calls and going inside a room alone just to talk. He didn't trust her at all, and she was acting real strange. Her ridiculous behavior was raising his suspicions. She was starting to make him nervous, and his antennas were going up because his spider senses had kicked in. That was why he was now sleeping with the Glock again.

Cee Money knew he was sleeping with his pistols. He knew he was sleeping with the enemy the entire time. And yeah, he also fell back in love with her. Why? Because the heart always outweighed the mind. You could never outsmart your feelings, no matter how much you tried to. Rednose used to lie to himself. He was in love with a snake. He was in love with the opposition. He was in love with the same bitch that tried to set him up, and if it wasn't for Ebony, he probably would've been dead a long time ago. So, now, he had to go back to the drawing board. Halftime was over, and the second part of the war was about to begin.

Chapter 7

Nya was ordered to pick three young girls. So, she had decided to take the chosen few of the students from San Diego State on a trip to the zoo with her. At least the ladies would have one last good time before they left American soil.

The San Diego Zoo Wildlife Alliance was an international nonprofit conservation organization that operated two world-class parks, the San Diego Zoo and the San Diego Zoo Safari Park, and empowered people to connect with plants and animals, develop an appreciation for nature, and contribute to the safeguarding of wildlife everywhere by becoming Wildlife Allied.

What always drew Nya's interest the most about the wonderful experience was that it never ever ceased to amaze her. All the amazing activities were so exciting. That was why she made sure she took a trip there frequently, at least twice a month... by choice or under some circumstances by force. It was the most beautiful place in the world.

With a focus on healthy ecosystems and the interconnectedness of the health of people, wildlife, and the habitat they relied on, San Diego Zoo Wildlife Alliance aimed to drive conservation outcomes benefiting people and planet.

San Diego Zoo Wildlife Alliance collaborated and partnered with hundreds of individuals and organizations worldwide to address conservation challenges utilizing innovative strategies. The Alliance synergized skills honed at the zoo and park with experience in the field to inspire and catalyze conservation action on behalf of wildlife, working toward a world where all life thrived.

Her family had been a part of this forever — the powerful Sanders family.

When she was just a kid, her great uncle, who also raised her when her parents died in a terrifying plane crash, was the first one to introduce her to the wildlife. Still to this day, he was the main reason that she would visit and learn so much about the zoo.

San Diego Zoo Wildlife Alliance was committed to saving species worldwide by uniting their expertise in wildlife care and conservation science with their dedication to inspiring passion for nature.

"Ms. Sanders, this is so amazing!" one of the students let out with excitement. The other two young ladies chimed in as well.

"Absolutely, it's my pleasure," Nya replied. The girls were so happy and busy sightseeing that none of them noticed how dry Nya's response was.

Nya received a phone call moments later. When she felt it vibrate, the palms of her hands instantly began to sweat because she knew what was about to happen. It was just like what happened last time.

Before she took the call, Nya looked in the air and caught a security camera staring directly at her. She was so nervous, just like every other time. She used a freshly manicured fingernail to remove strings of hair out of her face, an attempt to ease her nerves.

"How can something be so beautiful and amazing but yet so scary and dangerous all in one?" Nya wondered as she took it all in.

She couldn't help but to smile at the amazing environment while looking around.

The San Diego Zoo was a one-hundred-acre wildlife park that was home to more than twelve thousand rare and endangered animals representing over six hundred eighty species and subspecies. Located just north of downtown San Diego in Balboa Park, the zoo was also an accredited botanical garden, caring for more than seven hundred thousand individual plants, including a prominent assemblage of close to thirteen thousand specimens representing three thousand one hundred species. Nya used to take pleasure when she gave this experience to first timers.

Taking part in exciting educational experiences used to be everything to her. It gave opportunity and created lasting memories while supporting San Diego Zoo Wildlife Alliance's conservation efforts worldwide.

The expansive 3.2-acre Denny Sanford Wildlife Explorers Basecamp was designed to appeal to all ages and foster empathy for wildlife by exploring nature. Wildlife Explorers Basecamp, built on the site of the Children's Zoo, featured fresh and innovative elements, including eight buildings and habitats dispersed throughout four different habitat zones: Rainforest, Wild Woods, Marsh Meadows, and Desert Dunes. The area blended innovation and immersive technology with opportunities to check out extraordinary species ranging from leafcutter ants and orb weaver spiders to prairie dogs and sloths. There were interactive play opportunities, like a unique water feature with a seven-foot-high "floating" stone globe.

Nya was instructed to lead the three young ladies in this area. She was terrified beyond sensible thinking at this point because she knew what was about to take place, but she could not save the girls.

San Diego Zoo Wildlife Alliance's large membership base was vital in helping the nonprofit organization make a difference for wildlife around the globe and help build a world where all life thrived. San Diego Zoo Wildlife Alliance offered a variety of individual and household memberships with options and benefits based on the level of choice, ensuring everyone could become Wildlife Alliance.

The Sanders family and friends were responsible for more than ninety percent of all alliances and memberships. Of course, nobody outside of a special group of people knew this top secret G14 classified information.

San Diego Zoo offered beautiful outdoor and indoor spaces with sweeping vistas and lush, wooded areas that provided exceptional settings for any event from birthday parties and high school proms to weddings and anniversaries. By scheduling an event — large or small — at one of San Diego Zoo Wildlife Alliance's two conservation parks, guests were not only selecting a unique and memorable venue; they were also contributing directly to support conservation efforts protecting wildlife around the world.

Nya was very aware of all the special memberships and details about the zoo. Her family, the Sanders, were co-owners and had had a major percentage of shares in the company since she was born. A great uncle was the one who taught her everything about wildlife as she grew older. Her parents were killed because of their love for wildlife.

One day, both of her parents died when their privately owned plane crashed because it was supposedly overloaded with cargo containing animals from Australia and Africa that were coming back to the zoo.

Nya was adopted by the closest relative, which was her great uncle, Rui Sanders. Ever since that day, neither had become a part of the family business. What she didn't know until she became older was that the zoo and wildlife park were actually a scapegoat for what was actually taking place.

Her family had connections in Tijuana. The Sanders were involved with a Mexican cartel. Unlike the usual drug dealers, her family had no parts of the illegal contraband or narcotics. No, they were involved with something much more malicious.

All of a sudden, Nya took a detour from the original trail and began to lead the girls down a dark area, which was a blind spot for the cameras. The door had a small red sign with big, white, bold letters that read "Security Staff Members Only."

This made one of the girls raise an eyebrow.

One of the girls was white, tall, and lanky, one was Asian with jet black hair with a tiny body, and the other was a Black, intelligent looking sister that was cute but kind of chubby. She was the one who raised her eyebrow but didn't protest because she trusted Ms. Sanders.

The Black girl was curious because the hallway they entered was not on the agenda at all, but before she could question Nya, she felt a black gloved hand cover her mouth with a cloth. She was strong and a fighter, so she attempted to break loose. This only made the guy more aggressive. She tried to scream but only began breathing in toxic chemicals. The poisonous fumes kicked in immediately, and as a result, her body went limp. She was unconscious!

The same thing happened at the same time to the white girl and the Asian girl. They were all forced to inhale the fumes. Some other staff members stood on patrol as the girls were dragged to another private room. Nya kept walking as if nothing had ever happened and went out the exit and blended in with the crowd.

***

Ryan was doing better now and out of the hospital. While he was recovering in the hospital, a pair of nosey, husky cops came in to quiz him, but he lied to them with ease. He made up a story about some person trying to break and enter into his home. After a brief struggle, the intruder shot him then managed to escape.

The small handgun used by his fiancée didn't do any real damage. The only reason Ryan lost so much blood was because he had panicked and went into shock. Her aim was poor, but she had hit him a few good times in the leg. Ryan simply couldn't believe that Melissa chose violence.

She was tired of getting her feelings hurt over and over again. She was in love with Ryan before he became popular in San Diego. She actually thought he was a good person and had gained feelings. It was all romantic until he became famous and changed on her.

Actually, Ryan was battling a new drug habit, and this was what caused his random changes of behavior. Not only was Ryan dealing with insecurity, but he also felt like he had to prove himself in order to outshine the other up-and-coming podcasters.

The new social media world had everybody chasing clout. Everyone wanted to be a bigger person than the next. Ryan knew he was very talented and could entertain better than most locals who had millions of subscribers. Upon seeing other guys with less skills than himself getting more recognition, Ryan became jealous.

It was not because he was a hater but because he was better than other competitors who were getting more attention than him. So, instead of continuing to work hard and promote his talent, he decided to start using drugs, which was a bad choice. The worst part was that he was hiding the fact that he was an addict now.

The only person that knew his secret was Melissa. Instead of seeking help, all he did was have sex with 304 type women. This did not make his problem better. It only made matters worse. Ryan couldn't believe he ended up with bullet holes in his leg while resting in the hospital for two days. He did love Melissa and didn't want to hurt her on purpose. She apologized but didn't want anyone finding out that she was the one that shot him.

She was also the one who stayed by his bed the whole time he was in the hospital. She also promised not to call Rednose like she had been warning him. That would be messy, and she was a lady with class. She did call Nya to confide in her. This was a mistake since she had no idea Nya was awaiting any excuse to call Rednose.

Nya was thirsty but didn't let it show. Her spoiled ass was never told to kick rocks by any guy in her entire life. Rednose had been very casual and nonchalant every time she spoke to him. This only piqued her interest even more. She reported what happened to Rednose. He was polite and showed major concern but didn't extend the conversation any further than that.

Rednose was so busy getting ready to pop out of hibernation that he didn't give any extra energy to the situation. He couldn't do anything besides call Ryan on a FaceTime call to ensure that Ryan was okay. Before they disconnected, he promised to visit as soon as he handled some of his personal business.

Ryan did not know that Rednose knew as much as he did because he didn't speak on what was going on on FaceTime. The only reason Rednose hadn't really mentioned the rumors about Ryan on drugs was because he had his own drama going on. However, Rednose was upset with Ryan and knew that he would have to have a discussion with him face-to-face. Rednose's investment was governed by Ryan and his team. Rednose put a lot of trust in Ryan because he had known him for a while. Business was business, and Rednose was hungry for money, not a friendship.

***

Tijuana was a small city in Mexico that was right next to San Diego. The city was along the Tecate River near the Pacific Ocean and was twelve miles (nineteen kilometers) south of San Diego, California, U.S. It originated as a ranch settlement on part of a land grant (1862) and developed as a border resort with gambling casinos. In the twentieth century, it became the main entry point to Mexico from

California for American tourists, and tourism remained its most important economic activity. From 1950 to the mid-1990s, Tijuana's population increased more than tenfold. In the 21st century, however, due to gang violence, Tijuana was routinely ranked among the most dangerous cities in the world.

Rui Sanders was a powerful guy. He was the owner of maquiladoras (assembly plants) opened in the area beginning in the 1960s. He became known as the American restaurateur who moved his restaurant from San Diego, California to Tijuana so that he could consume and serve alcohol without fear of legal retribution.

Vast areas of surrounding farmland were opened for the cultivation of wheat, barley, and wine grapes through irrigation schemes, which contributed to the city's shortage of potable water, much of which was supplied via aqueduct from the Colorado River. The city was easily accessible by railroad, highway, and air from the southwestern United States, and there were many maquiladoras (assembly plants) that opened in the area during the 1960s.

The Sanders had several connections all across Tijuana, Mexico. There were business estates and real estate properties. Some were legal, and Rui Sanders collected millions of tax-free dollars each year. However, the most luxurious connection of all was a very private illegal operation.

This was an underground railroad that led to a kingdom of evilness. The Sanders were tied in with an unknown cartel run by the Mexicans. All types of evil activities were allowed for rich and wealthy people. These included prostitution, human trafficking, slave training, and a major organ donor ring.

Nya was guilty by association. She considered herself a saint, but she was the worst kind of evil — the kind of evil person who didn't think what she did was wrong because it would happen whether she took part or not. Rui Sanders had given her the best life ever after her parents were killed, so she felt like she owed him her loyalty.

She was simply in too deep. At first, she tried to run away, but Mr. Sanders had eyes everywhere. It was nearly impossible for her to just up and disappear. She couldn't escape San Diego without him knowing. Eventually, she became accustomed to the lifestyle. She lured in many girls each year to be kidnapped by the Sanders to be sold like cars to the Mexican cartel in Tijuana.

She did a lot of guilt tripping, which was why she started fundraisers and donated money to charities and pretended to care about all the missing girls in the local area. In fact, she had been the main character in setting the trap for the young girls that had been missing over the last few years.

Some of the victims came up missing during big events like college parties at San Diego State University. Some came up missing during late nights around the apartment complex owned by the Sanders family. The last three that were abducted would be known as an accidental death. Three girls that got lost and were attacked by two wild animals that managed to escape their habitat area of the zoo. The story would be that the girls were eaten by two large polar bears that became aggressive due to exposure to toxic pollution in the air; this would make the Sander's "anti-pollution company" gain more notoriety. Everything was set up to make more money; everybody was hungry for money.

"I can't do this anymore… I want a new lifestyle!" Nya cried while watching the news show three beautiful young ladies a few days after she lured them to God knows where. They were somewhere in underground Tijuana.

To make matters worse, Tyler would not stop harassing her. She needed a hero, but did she deserve to be rescued?

Chapter 8

When you thought of a spy, you typically thought of James Bond or someone or maybe Jason Bourne. But the real spies were the case officers of the agency, commonly called CIA agents in pop culture. But the CIA only called themselves foreign recruit agents, so a case officer was not a CIA agent. Because of the clandestine, sometimes covert, nature of their work, they were known simply as a 'spook' to many in the world of intelligence.

Devin was a menace, true indeed, but he was also very intelligent. So brilliant and guilty with natural skills that he could have easily chosen a better lifestyle for himself before becoming a malicious murderer. His skills were passed down from his grandfather and father. His family was very disciplined. On his father's side, they were all warriors — big, Black, strong soldiers at heart naturally. So, when it was war time, Devin had ultimate survivor skills.

Some people would consider him a coward because he fled while the deadliest shootout was going on. A lot of people he knew were killed that day, including his uncle on his mother's side, Ice Water. Yes, he ran, but now, he was back. He wasn't ready for war that day; he wasn't built for that type of environment. There was too much going on, and it all happened too fast. He just wasn't ready at that time. The loses he suffered that day made him the menace he was today.

Sometimes, he felt like his life had a bigger purpose than just being a foot solider in one mere shootout, just to die on one battlefield.

Wearing his usual combat outfit today, he was inside his van. Unbeknownst to anyone, he was trailing behind Ms. Trina. He had been doing this for the last few weeks. He even attended the small funeral for Randy. What was crazy was that he had been following the family since the video went viral. He had also been recording everything. He was going to edit it all once he decided he had enough to produce a psychotic documentary. He was spying on his enemies, awaiting the arrival of Rednose and Cee Money.

Devin was the only bad seed on his father's side of the family. The rest of his family were very successful. Most were in law enforcement or military affiliated. He was a nerd growing up. He was supposed to become a detective. He even went to school and got a certificate in the course of criminal justice.

Something changed inside him. He lost interest in becoming a good guy. After totally losing interest in school, he got caught up in the stupid street life. Sadly, this was easy when looking at his mother's side of the family. With relatives like Ice Water and other thugs, very bad influences, he became tempted and slowly started to follow behind them.

He thought the things they were doing were cool because they were getting easy money. The tip of the iceberg was that they all had a lot of fast girls following behind them. Devin went to school with those same women but had no chance of talking to them. Once he jumped in the street life and started collecting fast money, those same girls quickly changed their opinion. It took some time and a lot of money for him to realize that they didn't like him. They were just hungry for money.

"Where we-we going?" asked Coby, stuttering while sitting on the passenger side with a pair of dark shades on to hide his eyes. He was very insecure about his new appearance.

"We spying on Cee Money mother today and tomorrow and then the next day," Devin replied like a command officer.

His van was a few cars behind Ms. Trina's white Charger with the rims on it. She was straight ghetto fabulous no matter where she went. He even had to admit that she was holding her head up considering the heartbreaking situation her family was dealing with. She looked awesome for her age too. Devin caught a peek of that big, wide ass the other day, and his dick got hard instantly. If the circumstances were different, he would most definitely be trying to smash that ass from the back. He bet she had some good ass pussy. A wicked smile appeared on his face as he sped up to keep up with the accelerating Charger.

He reminded himself to stay focused. Devin was waiting on Cee Money and Rednose to pop out. They were not at the funeral. They hadn't come to the candlelight vigil. They didn't come to the party that was thrown at the new house. The city had raised money to help Ms. Trina move into a new house less than two weeks after her house was shot up. Devin had been spying on her daughter, Toria, too and knew she was out of the hospital and doing fine, but she was still in a wheelchair because her right thigh had tissue damage.

Devin had recorded a lot of footage of things that had taken place since the shootout. Pretty soon, he was going to record Coby's vocals on a track and release a video. He made Coby feel safe and had him thinking he was his security guard. Coby kept asking about two people —_his girlfriend and Ebony. He seemed to have forgotten everything and everybody else. Devin guessed that Coby was kind of Autistic these days. The motherfucker was lucky to be alive. Devin really didn't want to spill anymore innocent blood just yet, so he would give it a few more days before he committed act number two. For now, he was spying like a damn CIA Spook, hoping to catch Rednose and Cee Money slipping.

***

"So, we not going to Columbus... Never?" Keisha asked with tears in her eyes.

It had been a few weeks since Randy's funeral, and Keisha had gotten into several fights with her older sister, Cee Money. Although Cee Money was much older than Keisha, the girls were evenly matched in size. The wrath of Keisha's anger gave her unbelievable strength. She managed to get the best of her sister a few times. Rednose had to actually pull Keisha off his baby mama several times. Each time became more vicious.

The reason the two girls kept fighting each other was because they were battling for dominant respect. Keisha felt like Cee Money didn't care about the family at all. She felt like Cee Money was very selfish and didn't give a fuck about anybody but herself. Cee Money didn't have time to explain to her baby sister that the whole thing was a setup to lure her into a trap. She was too busy planning her next move. Until then, she knew it was best to sit still and be patient.

"No, bitch, we can't bring Randy back. You watched the entire funeral on video call, so it's just like you were there, so what's the problem?" Cee Money rolled her eyes and tried to storm away after speaking her mind, which she had been doing as of late. Cee Money was very feisty and outspoken.

"You ain't shit! How in the fuck you don't have any feelings after your mother's house was shot up and your brother got burnt alive? I'm glad my other sister didn't get killed behind your bullshit! I hate you! I should kill you my damn self!" Keisha had never used the word *kill*, so this got Rednose's attention immediately.

Before he could put his son down and restore peace, things got out of control. Cee Money slapped the shit out of

Keisha. Instead of fighting back, she went into the kitchen and came back with a big knife in her hand and began chasing behind Cee Money while crying and screaming.

"I'ma kill you, bitch! This shit all your fault, hoe! You got my brother killed, you slut ass, dirty, thot hoe! Stop running! Scary ass!" was all you could hear.

"Hold up! Hold up! Hold up! Yo, chill!!" was all Rednose could say because he was not about to get in between a crying and screaming Black woman with a knife in her hand. These two aggressive Pit Bulls were on their own. Rednose held his son's ears and protected him from the traumatizing scene.

Meanwhile, Cee Money ran faster than she had ever imagined to get upstairs and close her bedroom door and lock it behind her because she didn't want any smoke with Keisha while she had that big ass knife in her hand.

"Open up the door, bitch... Bring your pussy ass out here, hoe!" demanded Keisha while using the back of the knife to beat on the door. She was ready to kill her own sister, and she wasn't capping at all.

Rednose was scared now because he had never seen this side of Keisha. He didn't expect her to have this type of rage inside of her. He guessed the whole family had that dog in them. She looked like an angry Angel Reese at that moment —pretty and mean.

He didn't know what to do, but after a few minutes, Keisha just dropped to the ground and let the knife fall out of her hand. She started crying her little heart out. It was the saddest thing ever.

"Oh, my God, Randy. They killed my brother! They burned him alive... It's your fault... All this happened because of you. Both of y'all! I hate y'all. Please take me home. I'm tired of this shit. I'm ready to go. I'm ready to go." Keisha was breaking down like any teenager would. It was getting worse. Now, she was hyperventilating.

Keisha had been through a lot in her young life. She was very emotional and had been holding it all in for a very long time. Today, she finally let it all out. Rednose came upstairs and folded his arms and just watched her ball up and cry on the floor by his bedroom door. She was crying a little too hard for him. His heart melted. He felt sorry for her.

"Go ahead and let it all out because when we get to Columbus, we not doing no crying." Rednose broke the silence, surprising her.

Keisha's eyes got big as she looked at Rednose and jumped up and ran to hug him real tight. "Are you serious? Are you really going to take me to see my family?" she asked, sounding like a homesick child.

"Yeah, I think it's time, but first, you and your sister got to apologize to each other. We all need to be on the same page before we go back to that city of death. We can't be fussing and fighting with each other because we are all that we got. Cee Money, bring your ass out here!" Rednose led the two ladies downstairs where they all sat and talked for a few hours.

Keisha was just as famous as Cee Money, especially after a video with a link on Facebook appeared of a guy who snuck and recorded her while she was giving him oral sex a few years ago. This caused so much of an uproar. He said that he posted the video on accident, but we all knew that was a lie.

This humiliated the young girl and made all the guys look at her like a young thot, which was not the case at all. Actually, she had been in love with the guy. He was a jerk because he decided to use her feelings against her to manipulate her for his own selfish pleasure.

As a result of the video on Facebook, she was getting disrespected by all the bullies at school. She had to continuously fight a lot of times in public when being harassed by other females who called her out her name.

This made her an easy target for Coby's goons. With all that was going on, Keisha started walking from the school bus by herself. That was exactly how she had gotten taken. Rednose saved her life, and she had been living with him, her nephew, and Cee Money ever since.

Cee Money's reputation was not the best in the city either. Although Rednose knew it was all a big trick, the city looked at Cee Money as a used to be bad bitch that was now going out sad. Nobody had heard anything about or seen Cee Money since she was fucking with Ice Water.

So, she knew she couldn't just pop back up in the city like she had friends. Rumors in the street had gotten out that she had double crossed Ice Water and the RRG members — not once, but twice.

Rednose knew exactly what time it was. He knew those RRG members were going to recruit and retaliate after all the damage he had done to them. To be honest, he didn't give a fuck at all. Although he was ready to let his past lifestyle go and live a positive life, he was ready for whatever.

He did care about one thing, losing Ebony. He'd been secretly thinking about Ebony and how things went left so fast. He did miss her and felt bad for getting her caught up in his mess. Rednose reminded himself that as soon as he got back to Columbus, he would pay some respect by visiting her gravesite — just to say goodbye and give her the flowers she deserved. She really deserved more for saving his life and sticking by his side. What he didn't know was that he had a menace named Devin that was going to be waiting and lurking on him like a CIA Spook.

Chapter 9

Today, Devin was inside the van alone, just riding around on the east side. He had a huge smile on his face because the city was about to be cracked up. He'd just uploaded Coby's new single, *Stop Hiding*.

The video was so hardcore and malicious. It featured scenes of Randy being snatched up and forced into the van when he first got kidnapped. That was followed by Randy being held in chains inside the warehouse. Next was footage playing in slow motion of him getting knocked unconscious with the baseball bat wrapped in barbed wire. Next, it showed Randy being tossed out the van then set on fire with the metal blow torch.

The house being shot up while he was burning was so gruesome. There were scenes of Ms. Trina pushing Toria in a wheelchair at Randy's funeral, followed by Ms. Trina being spied on for days. It also had some clips of Coby's old video that he shot near the location where Carlos' body was found hanging from the tree. The video displayed so much violence and gained over a million views in less than twenty-four hours.

Devin had put old video clips of Ice Water and other RRG members who'd died last year. There was RRG Big Quan, RRG Bandlab, and other members who died during the war last year. Even the small team Coby had assembled got some airtime in the video. There were even clips of the original video director, Trey Vando, and some of the Gravedigger gang members. The video had some of everybody shown who was killed as a result of Carlos losing his life. The three girls who were killed during a shootout in the mall parking lot got clips in the video as well. Devin was really going to the extreme to get attention.

The main character was Coby of course. Each time, he was shown as the bad guy who came back alive from hell. He had on a weird looking Dark Vader mask and was holding pictures of Cee Money and Rednose as the song kept repeating "stop hiding" over and over. It was less than two minutes, but it served its purpose.

Once Devin uploaded the video to YouTube, he knew the fact that Coby was alive would shock the city. He would keep security on Coby and keep him hidden. It was funny how a song titled *Stop Hiding* would be the reason Coby would have to actually hide due to the GBI agents, local homicide detectives, and gang task force that would begin hunting for him. The video would cause families to relive tragic events. The community had still not received closure for numerous unsolved cases. The Feds were already arresting locals and sending them back to the streets wearing wires. This video would have so much attention, and Devin knew it.

Not only that, but the combination of Coby's team and RRG together was a twist that the city didn't expect. So, at the end of the video, Devin put his big afro into a ponytail then put a skullcap over it to hide himself. He also had on a black COVID-19 mask to hide his face. He explained that Coby didn't kill Carlos or Ice Water. He was only doing what Cee Money's baby daddy made him do. He mentioned Rednose but didn't know much about him, so he just made up lies. Devin was dry snitching like a motherfucker.

He learned new details about things from Coby. He kept him high and knew he was somewhat retarded since he was shot in the head by Rednose. One day, he came up with an idea to get hypnotized. It worked! This was when Coby began to spill all the beans about everything that happened. Even Devin thought Coby was the real deal, but come to find out, he was a fraud. He was only getting fame off of Cee Money's baby daddy's dirty work. Devin really began to realize that he didn't know who the madman named Rednose was, but he didn't care because he wasn't going to let him do him like he did Carlos and Ice Water.

Interrupting his thoughts, Devin realized he'd been drinking too much, so he ran inside the store to take a leak. Inside the van, Coby was high as hell, just chilling, and two of Devin's soldiers were passing a blunt back-and-forth in the back of the van. The van was parked between two other vans in a busy parking lot on the east side of town.

The shopping center had different stores like an outdoor strip mall. It was located off Macon Road. Inside the beauty store was Ms. Trina doing some shopping for hair and beauty products. Devin noticed that she had been doing a lot of shopping since she put on that emotional show during the protest. People had been giving her money she would've never gotten if he didn't make her go viral by humiliating her family the way he did. Lowkey, he felt like she owed him something.

"Hello, sir, would you like to try our new lemon pepper, juicy chicken, twelve-inch sub sandwich?" the bighead, tomboy looking girl standing behind the counter asked Devin as soon as he entered the restaurant.

"No, I'm good, shawty. I'm trying to borrow y'all restroom for one second then I'm out," Devin replied smoothly.

"Oh, okay, it's the last door on the left," she responded and went back to wrapping sandwiches.

Devin was happy he was the only person inside the bathroom because he had to piss and let out a loud fart.

"Wooooo, boyy!!" he whispered to himself while washing his hands. Devin splashed himself with some cool water before he stepped back out the restroom.

As soon as he did, the fresh smell of lemon pepper and cheddar cheese mixed with onions got his attention. His stomach started talking to him, and that was when he realized he was, in fact, hungry.

"Okay, homegirl, what you was saying about a juicy, lemon chicken sub sandwich?" Devin rubbed his hands together and approached the bighead, tomboy looking girl. She looked like she could fix the hell out of a sub sandwich.

"Yes, sir, we got all the best flavored sub sandwiches in the city. However you want it, I will make it. All I need is ten minutes." The tomboy looking, bighead girl flirted. She bit her lower lip and gave Devin that look.

She had that "boy, don't play with me. I'll suck the fuck out your dick" look on her face, and her lips were juicy too. Just when Devin was about to respond to her, the oddest thing happened. The door opened, and all you could see was a wide hip, big booty woman walking in, throwing her ass with each step. Ms. Trina sure knew how to strut her stuff.

She got directly in front of Devin, and his jaw nearly dropped. She had on a pair of the smallest white booty shorts he'd ever seen a woman wear. She was damn near naked. You could tell she wasn't wearing any underwear. Her ass was so brown and round. Devin was confused and didn't realize he was staring until she looked back at him. His eyes dropped to the ground in shame instantly.

"Excuse me, sir, did I jump the line? I'm sorry. I'm kinda in a rush. I got to get my hair done today, and my daughter asked me to grab her something to eat real quick. I hope you don't mind... Mister..." Ms. Trina had made her move on a damn maniac. What she didn't know was that he had been spying on her for almost a month and had terrorized her family. Her hot ass thought she had all the game in the world, but now she was about to get played.

***

Rednose and Cee Money drove in two separate cars back to Columbus. Cee Money and Keisha rode in the freshly painted, champagne-colored, drop top Corvette sitting on new Forgiano wheels. The girls were not fighting anymore but looked pretty as they drove down the interstate.

Rednose and his son were riding comfortably in his large, gray, Infiniti crossover coupe. His son was just chilling with his new pair of Jordans on, enjoying the music with no care in the world. Rednose was going to drop him directly off at his mother's house.

Although Cee Money and Rednose were going in separate directions, they had the same agenda. One would collect information while the other got a pair of ears back to the streets. Cee Money was going to be making calls while she and her sister surprised the family. Rednose was about to hit the city nightlife.

As he got closer to his hometown, he started to relive some of the good times and bad times. He used to be the man in town. Back in the day, he could pop up on any side of town and didn't have to have a weapon on him because it was all love. Things had changed so much since then, all because he got lost in the prison system for a decade.

Still to this day, he kept in touch with a few people he knew at Smith State Prison where he suffered hardship and traumatizing stress disorders. Inmates were still getting stabbed to death almost every week, and it was kept in house. They would lie to the public like always about how inmates were killing each other, and they weren't doing anything to make it safer. In the time span of seven months, two staff members were killed. One was stabbed to death, and the other got shot to death with a real live gun. When was it going to stop? This was why Rednose would never ever go back! So, he had to hold court in the streets if it ever got to that point.

Rednose's mind went back to the small city he grew up in. Columbus, Georgia. The population was only around two hundred thousand but had nearly fifty homicides each year. The rate was nearly one in thirty people were at high risk to become victim of crime, and things were only getting worse. Why was Columbus, Georgia so dangerous? Rednose had not been in town for a while now, but he had still been doing his research online and keeping notes. He was getting his information from the local online news websites. It stated:

"COLUMBUS, Ga. (WRBL) — The Columbus Police Department released new numbers from the end of the year crime stats for 2023. The yearly report shows murders are up from year to year; however, overall violent and property crimes showed a decrease from 2022 to 2023."

"Deputy Chief of Police from the Columbus Police Department (CPD) reported forty-five murders for 2023, an increase from the thirty-six in 2022 but lower than the historic high of sixty-six seen in 2021. However, CPD Deputy Chief of Police said there had been a significant decrease in aggravated assaults across the city."

Rednose had read online that according to the chief of police, the hope is that a decrease in violent crimes would eventually drive down the murder rate. While the numbers seemed to be trending in the right direction, he shared there was still work to be done to reach the overall goal – making Columbus safe.

"I'm not going to be happy, and I know the town is not going to be happy, until we drive these numbers way, way down. I am encouraged I think would be the better word. I'm encouraged seeing the overall part one crimes going down. I think with the plan we have in place, we'll continue to see that trend driving numbers down," stated a spokesperson for the Columbus Police Department. "We've got additional cameras coming in to be installed. We're using different pieces of software to manage all of the different technology,"

The department hired fourteen civilians, who would be doing jobs sworn officers did in years past, in an effort to help with the staffing shortage and strengthen partnerships across the city.

"Even one murder is too many. Stop the violence," a community activist had responded.

Rednose knew he was responsible for a lot of the crime in Columbus, Georgia, but he was not mentally stable during his first few months home from prison. Now, he was just playing self-defense and was not going to hurt anyone that wasn't trying to hurt him. Today would be the first time he stepped foot back in Columbus, Georgia. He, his weapons, and protection. He had a plan, and after he finally put an end to this second half of the war, he would move his family to San Diego, California. Or so he thought...

Chapter 10

Rednose had plenty of people to call if he ever needed to get the scoop on some things going on. Everybody ran their mouth like women on a reality show. It was so easy to find out who was who and who wasn't who. So, as Rednose saw his mother take Little Rednose inside the house and close it back, he jumped in that mode.

That street mode had his gun on his lap and off safety and very alert. He didn't stop at any red lights. The sun was down. He jumped back on the interstate, so he could get to the south side of town, avoiding more traffic lights.

He got off the highway on Victory Drive and hit the gas up the four-lane street. The smoke gray, large, Infiniti crossover coupe slid from lane to lane so smoothly. Its acceleration was incredible. In no time, Rednose was pulling up to his destination, the most ratchet and ghetto place in the city, Foxy Lady. The booty club.

The parking lot was packed with more stylish cars and trucks. Loud music and nearly naked women were all over the place. Rednose was here for a reason and one reason only. Intel.

He parked in the back of the club, so he could leave out in any direction. Right behind the club was a short street in the back of a small neighborhood that was slumped out. Directly next door to the strip club was another strip club. It was formally known as the Carousel Lounge but currently known as The Flame.

Rednose sent a text message to the girl he came to see. He knew her by her real name, Shantel Jackson, but everybody else called her Fun Dip.

A few minutes later, he saw her before she saw him. She was very little, standing around five feet. Her skin was golden with cute ink everywhere. She kept her hair done neatly and nails colorful. Her short hair style fit her round face and big nose. She would fool the average fella with her innocent voice and girly charm, but if you knew her, you should know better.

"Hey, my G. Oh, boy, you looking good, Daddy!" Fun Dip announced, checking out Rednose from head to toe.

Rednose's skin tone was a few shades darker from all the days on the beach with Ryan in San Diego and all the vacation time spent in the sun with his baby mother. He gained more muscle weight because he had still been exercising four days a week. His jewelry was up a few levels from years ago. He didn't wear many kicks these days. When you started getting more money, you liked to step out in Gucci dress shoes and Prada type designer loafers.

As soon as she got her little ass in his front seat, she immediately began filling him in on the street gossip. She talked for about thirty minutes straight before he could say anything. That was how most of those hoodrats in the hood passed information about everyone's business, running their mouth or posting on social media. All you had to do was just listen and pay attention.

"Oh, my nigga, I got something to tell you, but I don't want you to start acting crazy... I know how your temper is," Fun Dip said nervously. She knew by his calm demeanor and the way he sipped his drink like a player that he had no idea about the new video with pictures of him and Cee Money. He did not know that Coby was alive or that he was now sliding with the ops.

"What's going on, gang? Talk to me! If you talking about the video of my baby mama's brother burning alive, I already got the…" Rednose was interrupted.

"Coby alive! He got a new video called *Stop Hiding*. He linked up with them RRG members. They bragging about killing Randy. They saying they got revenge on you and Cee Money for setting up Ice Water. They saying Coby had nothing to do with Carlos' death. It was all you and Cee Money. Everybody looking for you. They saying you been hiding since you came home from prison because everybody wants that bag that RRG Quan got on your head for what you did to Carlos. I can't believe you haven't seen the video. It was on YouTube for twenty-four hours before it got removed. The Feds in town, and all fingers are pointing at you." Fun Dip was talking fast as hell, but Rednose didn't miss a word.

"So, Coby alive? Where he at?" Rednose said immediately, as if he was ready to go see if it was true.

"Nigga, I got the video on my phone... Look, this shit crazy, brah!" Fun Dip proceeded to give Rednose her phone.

Rednose watched the video twice and kept replaying the last part with the big, Black, husky guy doing all the talking. Rednose knew off rip that this guy was in charge of orchestrating everything around him. It didn't take long to see that. Now, Coby survived the shot to the head? That was just flat out unbelievable. "Wow, he survived," was all he said out loud but kept the rest of his thoughts to himself.

Fun dip already knew what was going on because she was messy and nosey.

"Boy, I already know everything, nigga. My name Fun Dip. All y'all niggas tell me everything I want to know when I get off that dick. My pussy is the best. Yes, it is. It ain't my fault that I fuck better than your bitch. I'm so fucking sexy." Fun Dip bussed her legs open and slid one finger in her neatly trimmed cat. You could get it splashing instantly.

"Girl, you funny." Rednose looked hard at her for a few seconds but knew she was a big thot, and he could never take a chance inside of her. She was like a public restroom. There was no telling who all had been in there.

"Where you going?" Fun Dip asked, noticing Rednose wasn't paying her any attention and was about to step out of the vehicle.

"I smell barbecue, I need me a plate." Rednose pointed at the food truck that was slanging plates like dope right outside the two ratchet strip clubs.

"No, uh, uh. If I was you, I wouldn't do that!" Fun Dip got serious, and her eyes were wide.

"Why? What's up?" Rednose quizzed.

"Them Gravedigger niggas in there, and if somehow them younger RRG members out here, boy, you in a opp zone. You'll be walking into a death trap. Niggas been talking about taking your chain when they see you, brah. It's not safe for you in the city anymore." Fun Dip tried to warn him.

Fun Dip didn't actually work at the Foxy Lady or Carousel Lounge, aka The Flame. She worked up the street at a strip club called The Gold. This one was the more ratchet out of the three. The Gold just didn't give a fuck. Those hoes were in there selling pussy on the side of the stage. A few would pull up in cars that had their Only Fans website link on the side. You could sniff powder and get your dick sucked for about $30 in there. The Flame had the sadiddy hood bitches who thought they were better than the other strip club hoes. Foxy Lady was the most popular. All the local, famous freaks worked there. All the rappers shot music videos there, so it was the best hangout spot for all the best dancers in the city.

Tonight, there was a party going on inside Foxy Lady, so all the dancers who worked at The Flame had stormed next door to get some of the money. All those bitches were hungry for money. They were funny because none of them liked each other, but when it was time to get money, they all stuck together. For example, on one side of Foxy Lady, you had all the Foxy girls standing together. On the other side, all the girls from The Flame stood together. It looked like a Mexican standoff.

Fun Dip didn't fuck with any of them hoes., All they did was fight over men and pass STDs to each other. She told Rednose that there was a lot of people inside and outside the club that knew how he looked.

"Looking for me? Snatch my chain off?" Rednose laughed at her like she was telling the funniest joke.

Next, he hopped out his vehicle and popped the trunk. He grabbed a designer bag and unzipped it. He stuck his hand inside and pulled out some more expensive jewelry such as chains, bracelets, watches, and a diamond choker chain. He took his time and put on all his jewelry. He also grabbed his favorite weapons. The two he could easily conceal was one small handgun he put on his leg strap, and the other was a very sharp hand knife he put on his right side.

"Hold up, hold up, hold up, boy. I already know what time it is! Please let me go get my shit and leave." Fun Dip gave him a hug and left as fast as she was talking.

Rednose just smiled as he threw on a black hoodie and stepped around the crowd of people posted outside by the food truck. After paying a few dollars to enter the club, Rednose let the security guard search him because he knew that the guy wasn't smart enough to find his two concealed weapons.

Foxy Lady was small, but it was always packed. Tonight, it was so crowded that you could smell it. This club was more than a strip club. It had gambling going on around the pool tables, and a dice game was in full effect. This environment reminded him of being on the big floor in prison. This was a death trap type of strip club. There was one way in and one way out. Ass and titties were everywhere. Rednose wasn't concerned about any ratchet pussy at this point.

"Heyyy," the cougar looking bartender lady yelled over the music. Her breath smelled like cigarettes.

"Yeah, let me get two beers... Any kind, it don't matter!" Rednose yelled and tossed her a twenty-dollar bill.

"Keep the change." Rednose didn't wait on a reply. He just grabbed a beer bottle in each hand and went all the way to the back of the club. He passed the DJ booth across from the bathroom and found an empty table.

He knew this was the dangerous area of the club, but he could see everything before it came his way. After a few minutes, he had completed a scan of the entire club. He knew niggas had guns. Almost everybody was carrying. As he figured, the security guard was just a front. He wasn't trying to stop anybody from bringing a gun inside. He was just making it look good by fake frisking.

"I'm trying to see who the fuck looking for the monster! Big Rednose! Not the little one! All that YouTube flexing, talking about *Stop Hiding*. Bitch, I'm outside! The real RRG killa! Solo driller! The biggest stepper!" Rednose started acting crazy and drunk while yelling over the music.

He took off his hoodie and held up his "RRG Killa" necklace. He began tossing money on a few hoes who ran his way after seeing all the water he was dripping in. The hoes thought he was drunk, but they were mistaken. They didn't realize he was trying to bait in a victim, so he could send a message to the streets that he was back.

It didn't take long before Rednose saw two niggas in the mirror on his right side. They didn't see him watching them, but he was discreetly watching them as they tried to sneak up on him.

This was a pair of young guys he'd never seen before. He could tell that they didn't know what they were doing, or they were nervous. Either way, they would be no match for the certified boogie man.

Rednose saw them talking to each other, maybe trying to debate if it was really Rednose. He saw one point at one of his necklaces, the one he wore while going live on Carlos' Instagram before hanging him. A few moments after that, he saw them reaching for their waists as they closed in on him.

"Damn, Daddy, you got that shit on tonight, boo!" one of the strippers yelled. She was popping her yellow ass all in his face. She was so hungry for money that she didn't realize she was about to be used as a shield.

Before the two street punks could make it to their weapons, Rednose went into attack mode. They fell for the drunk man act he displayed. He quickly grabbed a beer bottle and smashed it across the first street punk's head. With the speed of Jason Statham, he swiftly whipped out his knife and stabbed the other street punk in his stomach and leg while falling to the ground.

On the ground, he went for his leg holster and got his hands on his small handgun. When he glanced around, he saw over ten young street punks trying to get at him. He was trained for this type of pressure. "Let's do it, pussies!" He yelled and shot twice in the air. The shots caused the crowd to fan out. Everybody started running around wildly. The perfect diversion.

This gave him time to snatch up the high yellow stripper and use her as a shield. He heard someone return fire, so he stayed low. He made it to the parking lot and saw more niggas he didn't know. Something weird happened next. The guys in the parking lot were trying to get inside the club to battle the other guys inside the club.

Rednose didn't know who was who or what was going on, so he took this as an opportunity to jump in his vehicle and escape. He laughed as he saw a shootout transpiring in the parking lot. He wasn't trying to kill anyone. He just wanted to send a message to the guys surrounding Coby — the husky, dark-skinned guy doing all the talking at the end of the video.

Rednose wanted them to know that he was not hiding from Coby, Coby's flunkies, RRG members, or the Gravediggers. He was back outside and ready to play ball.

Chapter 11

Unlike his usual spy gate, Devin was not driving the van today. For the last few days, Devin had been chilling at the Motel 6 off Victory Drive. The motel was slightly across the four-lane street from the Foxy Lady, on the other side of the median. Normally, Devin would never be hanging out at the Motel 6. This one way in was like a big U-turn. It was like a hole in the wall. It was a big trap —_a scam hotel. If you didn't know anything about this side of town, it was best you stayed far away. Nothing was what it appeared. Everything was a big illusion.

The owner was affiliated with Big Quan, the one who took over the money affairs for the RRG members. So, all the strippers who worked at Foxy Lady and The Flame were working for Big Quan. He was the one who decided which stripper could sell pussy in the Motel 6. It was all a big set up. This was how Mook got killed. He fell victim to the money hungry bitches and got caught with his pants down. The Motel 6 off Victory Drive was simply a death trap.

Devin was immune to becoming a victim because he was a part of the trap. The only reason he was inside one of the rooms now was because of the freak off he'd been having with his new freak. She was a super freak. She had him doing the most, sucking her toes and all. They were matching each other's energy.

"Boy, I'm going to teach you a few tricks tonight," Ms. Trina said before kissing Devin long and hard.

He responded by gripping her big ass cheeks with both hands.

Ever since Devin and Ms. Trina officially met at the food place off Macon Road that day, it'd been on. It didn't take Devin two days before Ms. Trina was telling him she needed some dick because she had been going through a lot lately. The rough, hardcore sex she'd been receiving from Devin was all she needed. Ms. Trina was indeed a super freak naturally.

The first time they went at it, she let him pound her big, round, wide ass in the doggie style position. She was on all fours on the motel floor. Devin was on his knees deep stroking her. Each stroke caused her round ass to jiggle like Jello. Her pussy was tight for her age. She could even work her pussy muscles like vice grips. Devin didn't expect the tables to turn like this.

He was still trying to figure out how in the hell he went from spying on the lady, whose son he killed, to smashing her vagina walls. The crazy part was that he was actually starting to catch feelings for her. He had lost track of time and didn't realize how many days he'd been off duty. He had Coby surrounded by his team of loyal soldiers, so he was content knowing Coby was secure. They had the van with all the cameras and weapons. So, Devin stopped worrying and continued to enjoy himself.

He felt like he deserved a break from all the drama. He had successfully kidnapped Randy and staged a publicity stunt. He had Coby so brainwashed that he had no idea who he really was. He had produced a music video that had the streets talking. So, after thinking of all he had done, he figured a few days in some good pussy wouldn't hurt anything.

"I'm a suck on dem big, black balls with ice cubes tonight, Daddy," Ms. Trina said, licking her lips and giving Devin that look.

She slowly ran her hand over his black Levi jeans and watched his big dick grow hard through his pants. At that moment, she knew she had the young boy's head gone. Devin just smiled at her as he rolled up a blunt. He knew he was about to tear her ass up all night.

***

Rednose didn't tell Cee Money about what had happened last night at the strip club. He knew she was going to spazz out and call him stupid for doing a daredevil stunt. She didn't understand that he trained for moments like that. He always prepared his body and mind for battles and wars. Today, he was going to take Keisha and Cee Money to the cemetery where their brother, Randy, had been buried. Ironically, Ebony and her girlfriend's remains were also buried at the same cemetery. So, while the girls were paying their respect to their brother, he would do the same for Ebony.

Rednose obviously knew that he had no business going to the strip club on blind faith. He could have gotten himself killed. He still gave in due to his explosive disorder.

He was humble, even after his baby mama's brother was killed in the most humiliating way. The video Fun Dip showed him really sent him over the edge. Motherfuckers were talking about *Stop Hiding* like he was on the run or some soft shit like that.

What made it sound so bad was that Coby was alive and had linked up with the opps! He could not figure out this new generation at all. How could Coby's team and Ice Water's team be once killing each other, but now, all of a sudden, they were all rocking together like nothing had ever happened? They must've really thought Coby was like that. Rednose created Coby and knew he had no real heart. He was full of cap, capping about everything for a name, image, and likeness.

Fun Dip made things sound like it was really dangerous, but Rednose stayed dangerous. He had to send word to the streets that he was, in fact, not hiding. He was indeed back outside, ready to shoot some ball. In basketball, each team had twenty-four seconds to shoot the ball. He was shooting his opps down like basketball. So, why would he hide? He was just trying to change his life and live positively, but he saw that he still had unfinished business.

As he pulled up to the cemetery on St Mary Road, he circled the premise twice before parking.

"Come on, Keisha, grab all the flowers," Cee Money told her baby sister.

Keisha was so happy to finally be able to visit her brother and tell him goodbye. She was already in tears. Cee Money let her go by herself.

"You not going?" Rednose asked her, surprised.

"Why you flip the script last night at Foxy Lady?" Cee Money asked him. She took off her designer shades and folded her arms while waiting on an answer.

"What?" was all Rednose said with a clueless facial expression. He could be a good actor. His poker face was immaculate.

"Boy, my name Cee Money! I know everything so stop all this 'I don't know what you're talking about' stupid looking before I slap the shit out of you!" Cee Money told him with fire in her voice.

"Man, that shit wasn't nothing! I just popped out to send a message. Who told you about that?" Rednose was now staring in her eyes, watching for any eye movement that would indicate she was lying.

"Remember the day you came to my apartment and got mad because the guy was pulling off as you were pulling up? You asked me who he was, and I told you we did business together? Well, he was there and saw you in there acting up real bad. They said you was doing shit like an actor in an action movie. Boy, why would you put your life in danger without telling me, so I could watch your back? You know we are all we got!" Cee Money was in tears now.

She stopped crying and continued to rant. "My brother is dead, and you are the only person I trust to help me get back at them pussy niggas. We have to move smart enough to last. Cee Money will never get caught slipping. So, next time you jump on some gladiator shit, think about your son!" Cee Money rolled her eyes and used some tissue to clean her face.

She put her designer shades back on then put her handgun inside her purse as she got out the car and slammed the door before Rednose could respond.

"Aye, aye, hey, man! Don't be slamming my door... Big booty ass," Rednose screamed out the window as he watched Cee Money's booty jump up and down as she jogged in her tight pants to go catch up with her sister.

Rednose drove to another part of the cemetery until he found the area he was looking for. Moments later, he parked across the street from Ebony's gravesite. He grabbed two bouquets of flowers after putting his chrome .45 on his hip.

"I see you down there frowning at me... I know it took me too long to pay my respect. It's a lot of things that's happened since you were killed, baby girl. First of all, I made the nigga responsible for sending the hit on you pay with his own life. I made Cee Money snake ass seduce him and got him to spill the beans about how he sent two assassins to your crib, thinking I was holding all my cash there. Next, I found out where they were staying and shot them both in the head the same way they did you and your girlfriend. After that, I instructed Cee Money to bring Ice Water to an abandoned house where Coby had her baby sister held hostage. That's where I shot him in the back of the head and ended his life." Rednose got silent for a few minutes, reliving all the events mentally.

Before he started talking again, he looked around out of habit. He wasn't comfortable at all. He saw a car riding near the area, so he clutched onto his firearm. The car kept going, so he relaxed a little bit but not much.

"I don't know how to say this, but I'ma try to make it make sense. When you asked me to look out for Coby... well, I was looking to murder Coby. First of all, this nigga been dry snitching on me since the shit with Carlos. He was the reason you got shot up the first time — all because he wanted to argue on the phone with Ice Water. Now, I understand him and Ice Water was beefing over Coby's girlfriend before Ice Water killed her during a driveby shooting. It made no sense for Coby to tell Ice Water where the three of us was living at. Then, while you was bleeding to death, he was just standing over you, just looking. On top of that, he was going around the city telling everyone I was back out and we were the RRG Killas. This put us in danger. Coby had become a liability." Rednose took a deep breath before he continued.

"Finally, that day he attacked me and revealed that you guys were not biological brothers and sisters. Y'all had been lying in my face! He said y'all been having sex on and off with each other. Even when I was out. You just stood there. You didn't deny any of the allegations. At that moment, I felt betrayed. That's when I got back with Cee Money. Truthfully, I still had love for her anyway. I mean, she did ride with me when I was going through some of my worst times. Yeah, she tried to set me up for them RRG members, but shit, you crossed me too! I did not know who to trust. So, I went with my heart. I still don't trust her, but I do love her with all my heart. This part going to make it make a little more sense. Remember that day she sent me a picture message of a pregnancy test and you said it was fake? Well, it wasn't. Our son's name is Lil Rednose. I got a DNA test and all. He's mine. I got a reason to live now. I'm moving to San Diego in a few weeks. I just came back to take care of some unfinished business and of course to tell you goodbye."

Rednose didn't realize he was crying until a few tears fell on top of Ebony's tombstone.

Chapter 12

Devin had just woken up from another long night of mind-blowing sex with Ms. Trina. His phone started ringing over and over. He saw that it was one of his soldiers, so he figured something must've been important.

"Yeah, what's the problem? Yo, why the fuck is you blowing my phone up like you my bitch?" Devin asked, all grumpy. He didn't like being disturbed when he was enjoying something.

"Aye, Devin, we had him. It was him!" the solider reported, all hyper.

"It was who? What the fuck are you talking about? Speak clear. Now!" Devin ordered.

The soldier cleared his throat then began talking slower and more controlled. "It was the one that killed Carlos and Ice Water. We had him, brah." The soldier stopped talking.

Devin was up and getting dressed now. He put on his army boots and cargo pants. He fastened up his belt and put his assault rifle with the strap around his back. He looked at Ms. Trina and mumbled, "Be right back," before he left out the motel room.

"Listen, brodie, you're not talking in English. Stop tossing me around. Where is Rednose and Cee Money? Are you telling me that they are back in Columbus?" Devin yelled in the phone.

Outside, the sun was just coming up, and it was cloudy. It felt good, but Devin wasn't feeling the vibe. Something wasn't right, and he could feel it. At that moment, he knew he had been off duty for too long. He didn't understand what his soldier was trying to say to him. Before he could get a response, he saw the black van pulling into the entrance of the Motel 6. It went over the speed bump too fast for his liking. Suddenly, his cell phone disconnected, which meant that the soldier had hung up on him —_very disrespectful!

The van parked in the same spot that it always did, directly in front of the room. Devin was so angry that he wasn't thinking about Ms. Trina being right there in his motel bed.

"What is this? Nigga, you just hung up in my face? Are you nuts?" Devin was so mad that spit was flying out of his mouth with each word that he was saying.

He did not give his solider anytime to answer him. Devin was so strong that he only used one arm to snatch the solider out of the van. He started dragging his ass all over the pavement, causing skin to be ripped off his knees and elbows.

"Aggh, shit, my knee! Brah, you just made me buss my knee! Alright, man, I'm sorry for disrespecting you." The solider was in so much pain.

"Pussy nigga, don't you ever hang up on me when we discussing important issues, especially when you mention my uncle, Ice Water! Do you understand me?"

"Yes, sir!" the soldier replied, looking at Devin like he was crazy. He noticed the big assault rifle over Devin's big, broad shoulders, so he kept himself calm. Besides, he didn't want to get into a physical altercation with the big, Black, husky lunatic.

Devin's afro was flying in the wind while he was dragging the soldier all across the pavement, making him look even more dangerous. Finally, he regained control of the situation. The reason he lost his cool was because the solider was talking in riddles for one. Furthermore, he had mentioned Carlos and Ice Water, knowing that those two subjects were very sensitive. Devin needed some clear answers. He couldn't believe he'd been laid up with some pussy for so long that he missed out on some action.

"Okay, brodie, I apologize, man. I just miss my uncle, Ice Water. Okay, now what's going on?" Devin let out a deep breath then helped the solder back to his feet.

Inside the van was Coby, just chilling like usual with a pair of dark shades on like Easy E. He was always quiet and didn't interact much. Everybody just thought he was retarded. Three other RRG members were inside the van. Two got out and tried to explain to Devin what had happened to them.

"What the fuck? Who is this nigga?!" Devin reacted, looking at the two members that tried to ambush Rednose. He had to suppress his smile.

In a weird way, he was amused at how easily Rednose dealt with the street punks. He knew that Rednose was sending him a message. One of them had to get stitches to close his stomach back together. Devin knew a small knife was used to open him up like that. The other one had a big knot and deep gash across his forehead. They told him how Rednose slapped him with a beer bottle. Devin knew then that Rednose had seen the video and wanted to send his own message. He could've easily killed those two RRG members but chose to just send them back to the shot caller all beat up.

"Y'all talking about y'all had him. It look like to me he got both of y'all asses." Devin let out a loud laugh. Coby even chuckled a little, but no one noticed.

All of a sudden, Devin's motel room door opened, and Ms. Trina stepped outside. Before Devin could say anything, they locked eyes. It was at that moment that he knew he'd just fucked up. The truth was about to be revealed.

"Damn, she fine," one of the soldiers blurted out. Devin was too puzzled to respond.

Devin and Ms. Trina's eyes both glanced at the black van at the same time. Ms. Trina did a double take of the van. This was the same van she'd seen the day her house was shot up and her son was burned alive. It all came together right before her eyes. The big, Black, husky, dark-skinned guy with the afro. How could she have missed it? Was she that naïve?

"It was you!" was all she could say before she made a run for her life.

"Shit!" Devin knew he couldn't let her get away. He took the assault rifle off his shoulder and pointed in the direction Ms. Trina was running in. She was trying to get to her car.

Devin didn't want to shoot her because he had caught feelings for her since they had been having raw sex. He did not have a choice. He had to do something. He had frozen up for a few seconds, just like he'd done when Ice Water and Coby were shooting it out. That was one of the worst days of his life. He quickly pulled himself together and shook back to reality.

Ratatat-ta-da-ta!

Devin busted the stick at Ms. Trina, but she had managed to get in her car.

"Why he trying to kill the lady he was just tricking off with?" one of the RRG members asked another soldier.

"Crank up the van now! Let's load up... Chase behind her ass! This bitch can't get away," Devin ordered his team like he was on the battlefield.

Devin had put a few bullet holes into the side of her Charger but didn't hit his target. He ran back to the van and jumped in the back like Big Worm's shooters on *Friday*. That was when the pursuit began.

Ms. Trina was swerving over the speed bumps like she was on *GTA* trying to get away from the police. The van was creeping up behind her. Devin was hanging out the side of the van, trying to get a good shot to take her out, but he kept missing because she was swerving so well.

He knew that if she managed to escape the Motel 6 area, the black van would be no match for the horsepower of the Charger on the four-lane Victory Drive. So, he was shooting desperately but could not hit anything.

Ms. Trina was swerving so good that Devin almost fell out the van at one point. That was when he said, "Oh, hell nawl. Fuck this!"

Once Ms. Trina got on Victory Drive, she put the pedal to the metal and left the slow ass van in the dust. It didn't matter because Devin was the CIA Spook and knew all her whereabouts. She could run, but she couldn't hide.

***

Rednose, Cee Money, and Keisha were at the shooting range, getting some target practice in. Since they'd been back in the city, they had been staying in the Double Tree on the north side of town. The plan was simple —_find Coby and finish the job. Of course everyone else with him was going to get the same treatment.

Rednose was the type of guy who didn't trust anyone. His baby mother was his heart, and he didn't even trust her, but he was in love with her. He kept her close because they had something in common —_Little Rednose.

The child had stopped Rednose from killing Cee Money. She was supposed to have been dead when she crossed him for the RRG members after he murdered Carlos on Instagram Live. His son saved her, and somehow, he forgave her because he understood what she had said to him.

He had put her in a tough place. She warned him not to get involved with the Carlos situation. She had met Rednose while he was still in prison, so it was a lot that he didn't know about her. Cee Money ran with Carlos and the RRG members when she first moved to Columbus from Albany, Georgia.

Cee Money and her older sister, Toria, used to dance and trap for the RRG members. So, she knew that Rednose didn't have enough resources to start a war, especially with him just getting out of prison from a ten-year bid.

Yet he still went off emotions against his better judgement. This made Cee Money have to choose between her family's safety or remaining loyal to Rednose after he went against her. She chose to save her sister, but Rednose shot his way out of the jam.

Every time they tried to get the drop on Rednose, he would somehow always be a step ahead of them. Once Cee Money found out that she was pregnant with his son, she knew that she had to change her lifestyle. Going through the nine months alone was tough, and she was hurt when Rednose repeatedly rejected her until the DNA test proved that he was indeed the father.

Now, here they were, back to the bullshit. Cee Money knew Rednose would not let this go until his opps were dead and gone. So, she decided to have his back. She chose to slide with the man she loved. Carlos was the past, and Rednose had stolen her heart.

Keisha had to learn how to shoot, and she was not shy. Cee Money taught her how to hold her gun and how to aim it at the target's head. It wasn't long ago that Rednose had taught Cee Money; now, she was teaching Keisha.

"Yeah, that's right! There you go! Shoot! Shoot! Bow. Bow. Bow." Cee Money was cheering her sister on as she got better and better.

"Yes, I did it!" Keisha yelled, finally hitting the center of the target's head.

"I see y'all over there. Good job, ladies," Rednose yelled at the girls.

He was shooting a sniper rifle, getting his aim better. Rednose was already an elite shooter, but now, he was preparing for long distance head shots.

All of a sudden, his phone began to ring. He saw it was Ryan, so he took off his earmuffs and black gloves.

"My man, what's good, homie?" Rednose smiled because he was ready to move to San Diego, and he would leave the street life right here in Columbus, Georgia.

"Good news. We just finished the final editing of the movie. All we need is for you to hop on the next plane, so we can take some photos and set up the roll out." Ryan was very thrilled about the upcoming premiere.

"Congratulations, bro. We did it. We have come a long way, homie. Look, I have a lot of personal things going on, and as soon as I get ahead of my business here at home, I'll be on the next plane. I promise," Rednose confirmed for Ryan.

He was looking forward to getting back out there for numerous reasons. One extra reason was because of the sexy, young female who'd been texting him like crazy. Nya was definitely a hottie. He'd just been too busy to get at her like he wanted. Soon as he did though, he would give her all the attention she'd been craving.

Rednose wrapped things up with Ryan and was about to get back to shooting the sniper rifle until he heard Cee Money talking loud on her phone.

"What's up, baby?" Rednose asked her, sensing that something had happened.

"THEY JUST TRIED TO KILL MY MOTHER! COME ON, LET'S GO! IT'S TIME FOR SOME REAL TARGET PRACTICE!" Cee Money had that look in her eyes.

Rednose had never seen this type of rage in his baby mama before; he loved it. He knew it was time to get active!

Chapter 13

Cee Money had to do something about all this madness. Her whole family was in danger. Those RRG members really had her fucked up. Those niggas thought they could just kill her brother, put her sister in a wheelchair, and then shoot at her mom with an assault rifle. Now, it was her time to get in on the action.

Ms. Trina was tired of the ridiculous, out of control way of living in Columbus, Georgia, so she decided to move back to Albany, Georgia. After she almost got her top pushed back by Devin, Ms. Trina was petrified to even drive around town. She was also very ashamed of sleeping with the enemy. She felt like a dirty whore. She'd been sleeping with the man who killed her son. She was so embarrassed that she did not tell anyone. She just quickly packed her things and rented a U-Haul moving truck.

Her oldest daughter, Toria, wasn't feeling the same way. She didn't want to leave Columbus, Georgia. Nobody in Albany, Georgia respected her anyway. She'd been run through by all the popular guys in her age group. Plus, she had a man that took good care of her in Columbus. She wasn't in the wheelchair anymore, and her man was spoiling her very well. Cee Money knew there was no need in trying to convince her sister to leave with her mother, so she didn't even waste her time.

Rednose, Cee Money, and Keisha helped Ms. Trina pack up her property, and that was the last time they saw her. She was no fool. Ms. Trina was not about to become a statistic.

After plotting to herself for some time, Cee Money made some phone calls. She was using her cunning, conniving, and clever ways at this point. She implemented and utilized all of her resources to send word to the head member of RRG, Big Quan.

He was in charge now since Carlos wasn't alive anymore. Therefore, if the younger RRG members were on that fuck shit again, then he had to give them the greenlight. He had all the money and connections.

Big Quan owned the Motel 6 and a bunch of other cheap properties on both the south side and east side of town. Motherfuckers weren't just making shit hot without Big Quan's consent. Cee Money was the smartest person in her family, and she wasn't going for any stupidity. Big Quan needed to tell her something if he wanted to stay alive.

They never had any real problems in the past. The only time she ever had a problem with him was when she didn't tell him about Carlos beating on her and taking her money. Big Quan looked at Cee Money like a little sister; that was what she thought anyway. Truth be told, if he had ever gotten a chance before Carlos cuffed her, he would have tried to get some of that cat.

She didn't want to seem too thirsty or anxious to speak with him. Not wanting to ruin an opportunity after sending a reliable third-party source to relay a message with her number, Cee Money remained patient until he responded. It took two days, but she had finally gotten the call from Big Quan.

"What's up, Cee Money? I heard you been trying to get in touch with me?" Big Quan said upon her picking up the phone.

Cee Money paused, so she could gather her thoughts and control her emotions. She couldn't believe this nigga was trying to talk all nonchalantly as if he hadn't seen the video of her brother, Randy, getting burned alive. Instead of showing her true feelings, Cee Money decided to match his energy.

"What's up, Big Quan? How you been doing?" Cee Money replied with sarcasm and a fake polite voice.

"I'm good, shawty. How you been?" Big Quan returned a question back at her. He knew she was not stupid, but he wasn't either.

"I been doing fine," Cee Money replied, sounding like she wasn't going through any problems.

"Okay, Cee Money, let's skip the small talk. Why you back in my city? Are you death struck? You know I fuck with you, but your baby daddy is a dead man walking. If you want to live, you need to turn him over to the wolves, and we might spare you. Do you know how much blood has spilled because of this crazy ass nigga you fell in love with? You turned your back on us, on Carlos, for a nigga you met in prison! This shit is unbelievable. So, why are you calling?" Big Quan was talking loud and angrily now. He still wasn't over Carlos' death. He still had dreams of seeing him hanging from a tree.

"Look, Big Quan, you might not believe me, but after my mom almost got killed, I had to stop fucking with Rednose. I'm trying to get away from him now! He won't let me leave. So, I ran away. I need help... Please, Big Quan!" Cee Money was doing her best acting.

"Bitch, please. You are not about to set me up like you did Ice Water! You smart but not more than me," Big Quan said it in an *are you serious* tone of voice.

"Look, I know you don't have any reason to believe me or want to help me. I stole all his money out of his account. Me and my baby sister can meet you somewhere and I'll give all his shit to you, just please stop killing my family members," Cee Money offered. She was driving in her car with her baby sister, Keisha, on the passenger side. It was just those two.

"How much money you got?" Big Quan asked like he was hungry for money.

"I wiped his account out for over $70,000, but I need to keep something, so I can go on the run. I just need some help please." Cee Money knew the money was getting his attention.

"Look, you know I make $50,000 in my sleep, Cee Money. I'll tell you what I'll do for you. Give me all of that, and I'll let you and your sister come stay at the house off Clover Lane, but you can't tell nobody what's going on," Big Quan announced.

Cee Money rolled her eyes but bit her tongue. She knew that the girls who stayed in the house off Clover Lane were all junkies and call girls. Some were even street walkers. Big Quan was trying to take all the money and make Cee Money and Keisha workers. He didn't care about anything but money.

"It's nonnegotiable because you don't have nowhere to go, and you by yourself. If we going to do this, we going to do it my way. We will meet in a public area. I'ma have eyes everywhere. I don't trust you. You will get out the car and bring the money to me. Nobody touch the money but me! You and your little fine ass sister will get in my car and leave with me and my driver. I will count the money before we pull off. Do you understand? If you try to do anything funny, you will be shot to death. Both of y'all. I will have a shooter in every direction. You a sneaky bitch. Meet me at the old Walmart and Winn-Dixie parking lot off Buena Vista Road. You got about forty-five minutes. If you not there, I'ma come find you, bitch." Big Quan disconnected.

***

The old Walmart and Winn-Dixie parking lot was a large and wide-open area. It was built in 1989, located just off interstate highway I-185. It used to be a popular hangout place because of its large parking field with more than five hundred thirty parking spaces. It had multiple loading docks and access points. It was around 9.73 acres and had a lot of spaces.

The buildings there now were not as crowded with stores like it was back in 2013. It still had some buildings that were standing at around two or three stories.

Big Quan was riding in a black-on-black Mercedes Benz. He had a car full of shooters in front of him. Inside the Benz was Big Quan and his driver. They let the first car circle the premises at least four times before it double parked. Four RRG shooters hopped out carrying Glocks with switches.

They fanned out in four separate directions and held their positions, waiting for Big Quan to pull up. When Big Quan's driver parked the Benz, he jumped out and ran to open the backseat where Big Quan stepped out, looking like a slimmer version of Rick Ross. He was going bald at the top, so he wore an old school top hat that matched his dress suit. He really thought he was a modern-day pimp.

"Where the fuck these money hungry, trick ass hoes at?" Big Quan looked around the area and noticed how empty the parking lot was. It was so quiet outside that you could hear the wind blowing.

Big Quan called one of the shooters and told him, "After you see me get the bag of money from that hoe, kill the bitch and her little sister." Then, he disconnected.

A few minutes later, Cee Money pulled up driving the Corvette. She drove slowly around the Benz. Then, she passed the car that the shooters pulled up in but acted like she didn't see it parked. Finally, she parked way across the parking lot. She was in the open but far enough away to see anyone approaching. She left the car running and stepped out the car alone.

Big Quan was watching everything she did before she got out the car, looking sexy in an all-black, leather jacket and pants. Her hair was braided into a cute style. His dick got hard under his slacks and not because of her good looks. It was because of the bag of money she was carrying and also because of the fact that she was helpless, and he could take advantage of her.

"Tell your sister to step out the car!" Big Quan demanded.

"Here, get your money. She is nervous. We need to talk to her. She is shaking," Cee Money said as she approached Big Quan and took the small duffle bag off her shoulders.

She saw two shooters in the distance behind Big Quan and mumbled something to herself. Big Quan noticed she had a Bluetooth headphone in one of her ears. He got nervous and began to panic. That was when he pulled his gun from his waist area.

"Bitch, who are you whispering to? Drop the bag and get down now!" Big Quan took off his top hat and let the sun shine on his bald spot.

"Okay, okay. Damn, chill out. Why you tripping?" Cee Money asked him. She took two steps back and looked back at the Corvette where her sister had stepped out the car.

Cee Money looked up over the building and smiled then frowned at Big Quan. This confused him until he followed her eyes, then he saw a red dot pointing at his head.

"Nawl, fuck nigga, you get down! This for my brother, Randy!" Cee Money yelled just as a single bullet ripped through Big Quan's neck, causing him to drop his weapon.

Cee Money looked at Rednose, who was on the roof with the sniper rifle. "Good shot, baby," she yelled into her Bluetooth headphone.

All of a sudden, the driver did something very unexpected. After seeing the aim the shooter on the roof had, he decided to save himself. He smashed the gas, almost running over Big Quan as he laid on the pavement, choking on his own blood. The driver managed to escape.

While he was fleeing, Cee Money saw the shooters coming to aid Big Quan from different directions. Obviously, they were either too stupid or too far away to realize that Rednose was on top of the building with the sniper rifle and a telescope. Rednose had been practicing hitting a moving target for a few years now. He took a deep breath and relaxed before he took aim at the earliest moving target.

Cee Money pulled out her own Glock and shot at the other target as she ran back to the Corvette. She looked at her sister and was surprised to see her shooting at the other two shooters. They had already been on point before Big Quan and the shooters knew it. Rednose had been on the roof before they even pulled up. He knew the city like the back of his hands and knew all the shortcuts to get around town. He was even instructing her on where to park.

Boom! Rednose hit his target!

"Headshot, fuck nigga!" Rednose yelled as he saw his target fall dead. He was excited like he was playing *Call of Duty* and not in a real shootout.

One of the other shooters saw Rednose's target fall dead, and they all stopped chasing the girls and ran for cover. They didn't know where the shooter was picking them off from. The element of surprise was vital.

This gave Cee Money and Keisha time to get in the Corvette and jump back on the interstate. They weren't worried about Rednose because he had his own escape plan.

Chapter 14

Word had traveled around town that Big Quan and one other RRG member were both killed during a drug deal gone wrong. Rumors were misleading, and the story kept changing. Nobody really knew what had happened because when the cops arrived, the entire parking lot was empty. Only two dead bodies.

Devin was trying to figure out what really happened. He was also wondering why Coby was acting so weird as of late. Sometimes, he thought he heard Coby mumbling underneath his breath when he thought Devin wasn't paying attention. Once, he was fixing up Coby's drugs, and he thought he saw Coby trying to reach for a gun. When Devin spun around, Coby started acting all retarded. So, Devin didn't know if he was just tripping or what. Either way, from now on, he would be watching very closely.

Devin got a phone call from one of the RRG members and finally got the real details of what happened to Big Quan.

"It was that hoe, Cee Money! Somehow, she convinced Big Quan to meet up with her. The bitch even had a shooter on the roof. A real sniper! She was two steps ahead of him, Devin. Big Quan had me and three other shooters fan out across the parking lot. After Cee Money stepped out the car, she approached Big Quan with a bag of money on her shoulder. She must of did something that alerted him because Big Quan pulled out on that hoe and screamed, 'Get down.' Then, a bullet ripped through Big Quan's neck. That's when his pussy ass driver sped off. He even almost ran over Big Quan. We got into a shootout with Cee Money and her sister —_the baby sister, nigga! Then, when we heard a loud shot, we saw Lil Man drop dead. We was getting picked off! We had to get out of the open area. When we regrouped, they were all gone."

Devin didn't say anything. He just let all the information process. The first thing that he realized was that he had been underestimating Cee Money. She was not the same girl she was a few years ago. The second thing he processed was how war ready her baby daddy, Rednose, was. He knew the shooter on the roof had to be Rednose. Rednose was very interesting.

Carlos, Ice Water, and RRG Big Quan had all been like the big three of the group, Real Right Guys. Rednose had taken them all out in different fashions. The more Devin thought about it and analyzed his opponent, he started to respect his gangster. However, that did not put any fear inside his heart, only more rage and hatred. He didn't even know Rednose, but he didn't like anything about him.

Devin hated the way he took Carlos' bitch and made her his baby mother. He didn't like how he used Coby to be the face of all his madness. He did not like how he set up Ice Water and killed him so easily. He didn't like how he had kidnapped Carlos in front of his child. He didn't like how he had tortured him for months before he hung him from a tree while everyone was watching it live. He especially didn't like how he just sniped Big Quan from the top of a building like he was playing in an action movie.

"Who is this nigga, man?! Who the fuck do he think he is?! On all my dead homies, I'ma personally kill Rednose in the worst way. I'ma do it in front of his son too!" Devin screamed out loud as he drove the van on the highway.

Devin was about to say something else but heard Coby mumbling underneath his breath. Coby had on his dark shades like Easy E. He was still ashamed of his missing eye and scars. "Nigga, who the fuck are you talking to?"

"My-my-my-myself," Coby replied in the crazy way he'd been speaking since he got shot in the head by Rednose.

"Stupid ass nigga, you need to get your shit together because it's almost time to do what I been getting you ready for!" Devin yelled out because he was frustrated and upset about Big Quan.

He'd been getting Coby ready, so he could use Coby to lure in Rednose and Cee Money. He knew Coby wasn't ready, but now that Big Quan was dead, Devin had no choice but to increase the speed of retaliation. Now that Big Quan was dead, Devin had to figure out how he would get his resources and income. Big Quan kept RRG members financially advanced, but now, the members would begin looking for other means of survival.

Devin knew that without Big Quan feeding niggas, things were about to get ugly. Members would begin eating each other and crossing one another out. They were all loyal to Big Quan and his soldiers because of the payment and recourses. It wouldn't take long for niggas to become hungry for money and reveal their true grimy ways.

"Where we going?" one of Devin's soldiers in the backseat, holding an Uzi, asked, looking angry. He wanted revenge for Big Quan and Lil Man.

"To meet up with Big Quan's driver to see why would Big Quan meet up with the biggest snake in the city, Cee Money," Devin replied.

It only took Devin about thirty minutes to meet up with Big Quan's driver. When he pulled up to his apartment, Devin jumped out with the baseball wrapped in barbed wire. He didn't even knock on the door. He just used his size fourteen combat boots to kick it off the hinges. Once the door was gone, Devin forced his way inside the one-bedroom apartment.

"What do you think you are doing? If Big Quan finds out that you just kicked his driver's door in, you gonna be in big trouble!" yelled a dark-skinned, funny looking lady who must have been the driver's girl or something.

"Bitch, shut the fuck up! Now I'ma ask you one time... Where is Big Quan's driver?" Devin took a deep breath with his body language saying, "This is your chance to save yourself."

"Nigga, fuck you. I'm not afraid of you. You better get your ass..."

Smack! Devin interrupted her by slapping the vocabulary from her mouth.

Devin went on ahead and started choking her until she was dizzy. She tried to break free, but his hands were too big and strong. So, she bit him as hard as she could, and this was a big mistake. He choked her until she was now unconscious.

"So, you like it rough, bitch. I'ma make you regret it. All you had to do was tell me where Big Quan's driver was at, but you wanna be a bad ass. Okay, bet." Devin licked the blood off his bite marks.

Next, he looked around the small, one bedroom apartment until he found a sheet. He used his strong hands and teeth to rip it into long, thick strings like rope. He came back over to the dark-skinned, funny looking lady and began to strip her clothes off aggressively. She began to wake up and started screaming, "No!" This only made Devin more aggressive. The harder she fought back, the harder his dick got.

"Nooo! Stop! You hurting my arms. What in the hell are you doing to me?" she asked while struggling for breath.

Devin wasn't talking anymore. He just started moving fast, and he was serious. He first tied her hands behind her with the sheet he'd turned into homemade rope. He remembered watching a video on the internet of an inmate tie up another inmate with a ripped-up sheet, and he knew he wanted to try it on somebody one day. He didn't know that today would be his lucky day. He didn't plan this. She made him do it.

The more she fought him, the bigger his dick grew. Devin was creepy as fuck.

What really got him excited was when he stripped her, and he noticed she wasn't wearing any underwear. He figured she was probably in her mid-thirties. She had some big, juicy looking titties and a long, flat butt. Her teeth were yellow, but she had some cute hazel eyes.

"Ouch. Agggggghhhh." She struggled to move and breathe.

Devin had managed to hogtie her. He also tied some of the homemade sheet rope around her neck. Lastly, he grabbed a big piece of the remaining sheet that he hadn't ripped up and forced it into her mouth after he pulled the rope on her neck tight, making her open her mouth for air. He tied another piece of rope around her mouth to muffle her sounds.

She was moaning something underneath the sheets, but Devin just looked around the apartment until he found a plunger and belt. He began to spank her backside over and over again very aggressively. It was not in a freaky way to please her but in a psychopathic way to cause pain and torture. After her ass had whip marks, he finally stopped.

"Bitch, I should take yo pussy or even let Coby one eye having ass rape you! But I don't get down like that. You made me beat you into submission! Now, where the fuck is Big Quan's driver? If you don't cooperate, I'ma stick this plunger so far up your ass that you will be in tremendous pain every time you take a shit. Now, I'ma remove the mouth gag, so you can talk and breath better, but if you scream, I'ma pull this rope tighter until I strangle you. Do you understand me?!"

Spank! Devin had gone mad. He knew he wasn't going to be eating anymore without Big Quan.

The funny looking, dark-skinned lady shook her head yes. Devin removed the sheet rope from around her neck and mouth. She coughed up a bunch of yellow looking spit. She was sweating and looking at Devin like she'd seen a ghost. He was a menace.

"Go get my phone. I'ma call him right now! Please untie me. My back and shoulders hurt so much. I'm sorry. I'll do anything. Just please untie me. I won't tell nobody! I'll give you the best head you ever had, just go get my phone out my purse, so I can get his bitch ass over here!" The lady had an evil look on her face.

Devin just looked at her for a few moments. He wasn't expecting this type of reaction. Did his hardcore domination actually turn her on, or was she just saying anything to get loose? He knew one thing for sure. His dick was hard as a brick, but he wasn't a rapist. She offered some head, but he felt sick on the low but also turned on seeing her big titties bounce every time he spanked her.

Devin debated with himself as he went to get her phone. Once he got it, his mind was made up. Devin called his soldiers in the apartment but made one of them watch the front door since he had kicked it off the hinges. A nosy neighbor was looking at them until one of the soldiers lifted up his t-shirt to let him see the Glizzy and mouthed, "Mind your business, nigga." Then, the neighbor nodded his head and disappeared. The apartment was in a rough neighborhood, so this wasn't anything surprising to most neighbors. That neighbor had grown up in Columbus, Georgia and knew it was safer to mind your own business.

Back in the apartment, Devin had untied the lady but left the sheet rope around her neck. He made her crawl like a slave dog bitch and suck three different dicks, one at a time. She had to taste three different men's sperm in one day. She had offered to do anything, and she swallowed all the cum with no complaints. She was spitting and choking on the dicks like she enjoyed them and had been waiting a lifetime to get slutted out. She went from being a victim to becoming a willing participant. Such a fucking whore. Disgusting!

Chapter 15

It wasn't hard to put together a plan for Big Quan's death trap. Cee Money knew he was an easy target because he was a tender dick ass, money hungry nigga. She also knew he had a sweet spot for her, and she could persuade him to meet up with her if he felt like she was vulnerable. Now he was a dead man.

"Baby, all that target practice from long distance really got your sniper game elite," Cee Money told Rednose before kissing him on the lips.

"Nawl, did you see Keisha?! Man, that's my little shooter!" Rednose went on to brag about how she jumped out the car and shot at the opps like a real shooter. Even though she didn't hit anybody, she made them fan out and run for cover. That gave Cee Money the opportunity to escape without getting hit up.

"Yes, she did good, but did you see me bussing my gun, baby?" Cee Money asked, obviously jealous of her baby sister.

"Baby, I been training you for a few years now, so I expect you to be a good shooter. You did exceptionally well." Rednose smiled at Cee Money.

Cee Money just rolled her eyes as if to say, "Yeah, whatever." They had the type of bond where they would know what the other one was thinking without saying much. They could feel each other's energy and knew what certain body language meant. Rednose knew that Cee Money didn't like that her sister was being praised by her baby daddy. Although she wasn't showing it, Rednose knew that Cee Money was still very upset at her sister for pulling a knife out on her. So now that she knew how to shoot a handgun better than any other teenage girl, Cee Money knew it would be trouble if they were to face off again.

Rednose, Cee Money, and Keisha were back at home in Riverdale, Georgia. They had taken Cee Money's older sister, Toria, some cash, a pistol, and some pepper spray for protection because she was the only one left from her family still in Columbus, Georgia. She was staying with some guy who claimed he loved her with all his heart and would keep her safe.

After the shootout transpired in the old Walmart parking lot, Rednose left his own message as a response to Coby's diss song, *Stop Hiding*. Before they left, Rednose went back to the parking lot with some green air brush paint. He made the letters big and bold. They were about thirty feet wide. They read, "Now Who Hiding?"

***

With nowhere to run to, Big Quan's driver finally decided to go home. When he pulled up to the apartment, he had his head down, looking at his phone. So, he really wasn't paying attention. When he did look up, he saw that his door had been kicked off the hinges, and he panicked and tried to run back to the car, but somebody had gotten behind him with a Draco, aiming at his back. He looked to his left and saw another RRG member aiming a stick at him. He looked to his right and saw another gun pointing at him.

"Get your bitch ass over here, scary ass, punk motherfucker!" Devin yelled, not waiting for him to get closer.

He snatched him up and started dragging him inside the small apartment. When the driver looked at his girl just sitting there with cum on her face and scared to move, he knew her freaky ass had gotten turned out by the members. She was a nympho, slut hoe anyway. All anyone had to do was get aggressive with her, and she would become extremely horny. He tried to keep her to himself because he took her from another loser, but now, Devin was about to take her from him and put her big tittie ass in one of the houses off Clover Lane.

"Bitch, you in here sucking niggas' dick or some shit? What the fuck is that on your face?" The driver was so mad that he'd rather start an unnecessary argument with her than bargain for his life.

"I sure did," was all she said, looking like a thot hoe.

"Bitch, I'ma kill you…"

Whack! Devin slapped him across the head with the baseball bat wrapped in barbed wire, cutting him off.

A few minutes later, the driver was asking where he was and how he'd gotten here. That bat was the real deal.

"Listen, bitch nigga, I'ma ask you a few questions, and if you don't give me the answers I want, I'ma have some fun with you before I kill you. Look, I know that you left Big Quan when he got sniped down, but I don't know why would you do something so stupid if you knew you would have to deal with me? The real question is why did Big Quan meet up with Cee Money without calling me?" Devin snatched him up and sat him down on the La-Z-Boy.

It took the driver a few minutes to get himself together. He looked at his girlfriend, who'd just gotten done sucking three different dicks like he wasn't going to kill her if he survived this ordeal.

"Cee Money tricked him. I told that nigga not to trust that bitch, but he didn't listen to me. She fed him some bull crap about how she was on the run from Rednose. She claimed she wiped her baby daddy, Rednose, for $70,000 and was willing to pay Big Quan to protect her from him because he was going to kill her if he found out. She said her sister, the one who went viral for sucking dick on Facebook, was even with her, and they both would do anything for security. So, Big Quan offered to hide them inside one of the houses off Clover Lane and make them hoes work, but they couldn't tell nobody. That's why he didn't call you because he knew you would kill the bitch for setting up your uncle, Ice Water," the driver said truthfully because he didn't give a fuck about anything at this point. All he wanted to do was get his hands on the funny looking, dark-skinned lady with the big titties.

Devin just shook his head and let all the information process that he had just received. He knew that Big Quan's driver wasn't lying about anything he said. That was the only thing that made sense. Devin was the strongest muscle that the RRG members had, so why not call him to get revenge for Ice Water and Carlos? Because that freaky ass nigga wanted to beat Cee Money's pussy up and probably get some head from her underaged, fine ass sister. Big Quan was dumb as fuck. He just went out so bad.

"Where the seventy grand at?" Devin asked the driver while staring at him, looking for any signs of hesitation.

"She never even showed the money. This bitch, Cee Money, has stepped her game up. The whole thing was a set up. We thought we were the first ones to get to the parking lot, but they had been way ahead of us. Cee Money had a real sniper on the roof and was talking to him from her headset. Devin, no cap, brah! The shit gave me chills and reminded me of some *Call of Duty* type shit. Whoever her baby daddy is must be some Navy SEAL nigga. I swear he picked Big Quan's ass off from long distance. He is not your typical street nigga. Y'all better be ready to face off with these two because they making this shit look easy." The driver looked around at the other RRG members who were standing around Devin with assault rifles and handguns.

The driver was trying to let them know that Rednose was on another level. He didn't care what happened to these niggas. They had just kicked in his door and somehow turned his bitch against him, so now he didn't care what he said to Devin and the members. At this point, whatever was going to happen was going to happen regardless.

Devin just started scratching his big afro because he was getting nervous but tried to contain himself. He couldn't believe that Rednose just popped up and kidnapped Carlos like he was nobody. Carlos ran the whole city and was the leader of RRG. Not only did he kidnap him and torture him, but he also murdered him viciously and hung him from a tree while Carlos' Instagram was going live.

Rednose killed Ice Water like he was a random flunkey. Some kind of way, this nigga, Rednose, had brainwashed Cee Money because she, at first, tried to set him up for Ice Water and the members to get him to reveal where Carlos was, but he transformed her character and made her do the opposite — set up Ice Water for Rednose to kill him.

Then, the nigga found out about the video that Devin put together, joining Coby's team and reuniting RRG. Instead of making Rednose look bad, he reversed that situation. He walked in the middle of Big Quan's event at a strip club and injured two RRG members just to send a message to Devin and Big Quan.

Devin failed at trying to kill Cee Money's mother. Cee Money retaliated by conning Big Quan because he owned the Motel 6. This all made Devin kind of nervous. He had to admit that he had not only underestimated Rednose but Cee Money too. He knew it was time to set up the final act and make Coby bring them both out for the final shootout. It was going to be a sudden death match. Devin would kill Cee Money, Rednose, and Coby. This was the only way he would feel like he'd gotten justice for the RRG members.

"Last question, buddy. Where you went after you left Big Quan for dead?" Devin asked, and for the first time, the driver's eyes got big, and his hesitation confirmed what Devin already knew.

Devin knew that only Big Quan's driver knew all the spots where Big Quan kept all the weekly money that he collected from everyone on each side of town. He was the driver, so he saw everything and knew where to go to get all the large amounts of cash.

"I just left because I didn't want to die! I told that nigga not to trust that bitch. He wasn't even that worried about the money. He kept talking about how thick and big her ass had got since she had the baby. Man, I left. I got my own life to protect," the driver admitted, hoping Devin would understand.

Devin thought about when he ran from the shootout that took Ice Water's life, so he couldn't act like he did not feel where the driver was coming from, but the driver was leaving something out. He must've thought that his good talk game worked.

All of a sudden, Devin went outside and peeped inside the driver's car. Next, he opened the front door and popped the trunk.

"Jackpot!" Devin closed the trunk back before any of the other RRG members came outside. He didn't plan on sharing the money with anyone else.

"Okay, so you can keep a secret, cool. I can also. Now, your bitch don't wanna be with you anymore because you about to be broke and can't take care of her money hungry ass. So, she is about to leave with us, and you will never attempt to reach out to her again. Here, this is about $1,700 cash. This should pay for your front door to be repaired. The car is also leaving with us. Big Quan paid for it. Only thing you keep is this musty ass apartment and your life. You lucky I'm letting you live. I should push your wig back right now, but I'ma spare you for a few reasons. The main reason is because I understand why you left Big Quan for dead." After saying that, Devin winked his eye at Coby and then he smiled.

One of the shooters got in the driver's car with the funny looking, dark-skinned lady. Devin got in the backseat to stay close to all the money that only him and the driver knew about. The rest of the crew was going to come behind them in the black van. They would all meet up at one of the houses off Clover Lane.

"Why you still in my apartment, funny looking ass nigga? Devin's in charge now. You heard what the fuck he just said. Nigga, I live. So, get your retarded looking ass out my shit," the driver yelled at Coby.

Coby looked around to make sure nobody could hear him before he finally stopped role playing. "See, that's y'all problem. Y'all so stupid. Y'all think everyone retarded. So smart that y'all dumb. Look at my face, nigga." Coby took off the head scarf and removed the eye patch.

"Ewwww, what the fuck happened to you, mannn? I'ma throw up! You look like Freddy Krueger, mannn!" The driver had a sense of humor, but Coby was a serial killer who could role play for his own personal plans.

"Oh, don't worry. You about to look just like me, my G," Coby said, sounding just like Rednose used to.

Coby kicked the driver directly in his face then pulled out a knife. Rednose had taught him how to handle all kinds of small weapons. He said that the easy to conceal weapons were the best ones to use. Coby went to work on the driver's face, cutting around his left eye socket like he was carving a pumpkin. Blood splattered everywhere. When he was finished, he had the driver's eye in his hand.

"Now go look in the mirror and throw up because we both look like twins now, mannn," Coby said, using the voice the driver had been talking in. Coby was such a good actor.

He went in the bathroom to wash all the flesh and blood off his hands. Then, he cleaned his knife off. Before he went back to the van, he put back on his head scarf and eye patch. One of the RRG members met him in the hallway.

"Bring your retarded ass on. Devin wants you to get some practice in before we set up the final shootout," the member said.

"Oh-oh, okay. I'm-I'm ready," replied Coby, back stuttering and walking with a phony limp.

Chapter 16

Departing from Hartsfield-Jackson Atlanta International Airport (ATL)

Arriving at San Diego International Airport (SAN)

Average flight time: 4 hours 18 minutes

Distance: 1,892 miles

Cee Money was so jealous that Rednose allowed Keisha to get on the plane with them. She was hoping to get some privacy with her boo for the few days they were going to be in San Diego, California. She was sick of Rednose treating Keisha like a little spoiled brat. Nobody ever treated her like a baby when she was growing up. She had it hard, and her older brother, Randy, never came to her rescue.

"This is not a vacation. I'm just going to grease some palms, and I'm out. However, if you insist on boarding the plane with me, you might as well get three tickets because Keisha is coming also," Rednose told her when she sat on his lap and tried to kiss him into saying yes. She knew her sister was becoming a problem and needed to find a life or something.

Now that they had landed in San Diego, California, Cee Money went online and read about the best tour guide around town. She wanted to go get her toes in the beach. Keisha wanted to go visit the zoo like a little ass kid. Cee Money ignored her sister's excited voice and read all the unique things and places about San Diego, California.

"Nestled along the southern shores of California's Pacific coastline, San Diego is a city steeped in more than just white sand beaches and sunshine. Known for its sprawling green parks, bayfront views, and vibrant streets, it's a city you'll want to spend far more than just a few days in.

"Having just arrived on your first San Diego trip, you'll want to get started on learning everything about it. From trying out some must-see experiences to following a trusty San Diego tour guide around some of the city's most well-known historical hotspots and hidden gems, your first visit to San Diego is sure to be a magical one. Make sure you get the most out of your San Diego trip by exploring with Old Town Trolley Tours, who will take you from A to B in the most exciting, smile-inducing way —_featuring all these must-see San Diego sights and so much more.

"As the city that has it all, it can often feel impossible to decide which San Diego attractions to tick off your list, but there are a few San Diego sights that are a must. No first-time visitor's guide to San Diego is complete without a trip to San Diego Zoo —_the perfect way to start your day before moving on to explore America's largest cultural park, Balboa Park, and take in the colorful sights of San Diego's lively downtown. As your trip moves on, you'll take in many San Diego attractions, such as scenic Seaport Village and the ocean views of La Jolla and San Diego Bay. All these sights can be seen to their fullest with a San Diego tour guide by your side. This might be your first visit to San Diego, but it won't be the last.

"The number one stop on any visitor's guide to San Diego, especially if it's your first visit, San Diego holds deep pride in its city zoo, which is spread over 100 acres of verdant land filled with over 3,000 animals and 800 species from all corners of the globe. Hop on here as your first stop with Old Town Trolley Tours and spend hours winding between each point. Elephant lovers will be enchanted by Elephant Odyssey and both children and adults alike by

Koalafornia and the Children's Zoo. When hours have passed here, hop back on the trolley to explore the next of your San Diego sights.

"Far more than your usual city park, Balboa Park is San Diego's crowning jewel. Also known as "the Smithsonian of the West", this San Diego trip-maker encompasses over 1,200 acres of museums, theater venues, and beautiful botanical gardens, a true oasis away from the bustling vibe of the city. During your first visit to San Diego, make the Natural History Museum and Japanese Friendship Garden a must —_with the help of the San Diego tour guide on your Old Town Trolley Tour.

"As memorable at night as it is during the day, Downtown San Diego is the beating heart of the city. Never missing from any visitor's guide to San Diego, it's a place to shop, eat, dance, and come together —_from dawn till dusk, young to old. Your San Diego tour guide may suggest making two stops here: one for shopping and people watching at Horton Plaza during the day and another for dining out in the iconic Gaslamp Quarter in the evening. This buzzing San Diego attraction captures the hearts of everyone and offers everything from family-friendly food spots to artsy boutiques you can happily get lost in. Whatever your style, you'll quickly find there's something on this San Diego trip for everyone.

"Seaside cities call for sea views, and San Diego is no exception. On your first visit to San Diego, you may find yourself gravitating towards the bayfront gem of Seaport Village. Opened in 1980, it's quickly become one of the must-see San Diego sights on everyone's list. Lunch, learning, or simply strolling by the water, this shopping and dining complex has everything from galleries to smoothie stalls, offering a unique experience overlooked by beautiful oceanic views. Hop off here when you're looking for a break from the midday sunshine and a bite to eat at one of many eclectic (but moreish) eateries.

"While many know San Diego sights as stretching out to sea, you can also catch sparkling city views when visiting San Diego Bay. A natural harbor and maritime history hotspot, it's the perfect place on your San Diego trip to stop and smell the sea air. Take in many parts of this must-see San Diego sight with a San Diego tour guide, and if you're after a little more adventure, why not try a cruise around North Bay or South Bay? Whether it's for a sunset dinner or a whistle-stop tour, it's one San Diego sight you won't want to miss.

"A big favorite among locals and tourists alike, whale watching can't be missed by any visitor's guide. San Diego is home to some of the best Pacific Ocean views in the country — which means even more opportunities to see whales swimming majestically in their natural habitat. If you're basing your San Diego trip around which whales and dolphins you'd like to see, note that sightings are seasonal; those wishing to catch sight of the elusive blue whale would love to visit."

Cee Money was going to spend some money on her and her spoiled ass sister, she supposed, while Rednose was going to meet up with his team on the other side of town. She would take her sister to the zoo, but first, she was going to put her toes in the sand. She had been standing on business; now, she was about to stand on the beach.

***

Rednose and Ryan were acting pretty normal for two guys that were on the red carpet with some A-list actors and actresses. Ryan looked like he was a celebrity already. He just had that star appearance and knew he was the one. Rednose could have his asshole, arrogant moments; today was one of his moments.

They were there for the world premiere of Ryan's new film, *The Time Stopper Man*. Rednose had written the film idea while he was in prison. Today was the first time that people actually got to meet and greet Rednose. Ryan had been telling everyone how incredibly skilled he was with his pen. They stayed at the venue for over four hours, and Rednose was ready to leave. He hadn't seen Cee Money all day, and he missed her. He couldn't wait to get back to the five-star hotel, where the room was on the top floor, and fuck her on the balcony while looking at the skyscrapers in the night light.

"So, let's talk about you using drugs, Ryan," Rednose said to Ryan once they finally left and got into the back of a limousine.

Ryan was so caught off guard that he just let his jaw drop like he was in the middle of an action scene. He went on to explain to Ryan that the cute girl, Nya, had told him why Melissa had shot him up. He also told Ryan that they were cool before they started doing business together.

"I used to have a bad drug habit also, Ryan, but I overcame my addiction. I had to just put my mind to it, and I went cold turkey one day out of nowhere. Drugs will make you do crazy things, and you will regret it when you snap back to reality. It's only a temporary scapegoat. The more you use them, the more you need. There is no good ending. Trust me." Rednose was talking to Ryan like an older brother and not his boss that cut his paychecks.

Ryan broke down when Rednose put his hands on his shoulder. He cried without saying a word for a few minutes. He gathered himself and looked at Rednose.

"Man, I can't do all this by myself out here. All the girls and followers think I'm rich and famous. It's hard to keep up that image, bro. I don't want you to think I can't handle business —I got it —I just wish you was here with me. I don't really trust the other team members outside of work. I mean, they are cool, but they are lame as fuck with no personal lives. I be bored, and my girl, Melissa, is my everything. The only reason I cheat on her is just to keep up the playboy image." Ryan was keeping it real with Rednose and speaking from the heart.

"I understand, my G. I truly do. Look, you been doing good. The whole team is about to get a pay raise, and you don't have to worry about being alone too much longer because I'm moving to San Diego in less than a month. Me and my baby mother." Rednose smiled then popped a bottle of champagne.

***

Nya saw Rednose on the red carpet, and her panties got moist so fast that she was embarrassed and had to excuse herself. When she came back to the VIP section where all the popular people decided to hangout, he and Ryan had disappeared into the crowd. This didn't stop Nya because she was so determined to get what she wanted. She made some calls and learned that Rednose and his podcast members were having dinner at Island Prime.

Located on Harbor Island, Island Prime offered stunning views of the San Diego Bay, downtown skyline, and Coronado Bridge. The main dining room showcased floor-to-ceiling windows and was propped up on wooden stilts over the water, making it the only waterfront steakhouse in the city of San Diego.

Nya walked into the restaurant like she owned the place. Her last name was Sanders, and they ran this town, like that song Jay-Z and Rihanna used to sing. She had on an all-pink, body-hugging, Prada dress with some open toe sandals to match. She was looking very wealthy and lavish. She sat at a section by herself until she saw him. Rednose was looking so good to her. He had even switched his outfit and was wearing a dark, two-piece suit with a bow tie. When they made eye contact, Rednose made his way to her.

"So, you just going to sit in the corner and watch me like you my parole office?" he joked as he sat next to her and kissed her soft hand.

"How do you know I'm not here with anybody else?" she asked, looking all shy.

"Because I saw you come in here. I don't miss anything. I watch my surroundings very careful, especially when I'm out of town," he replied.

They spoke to each other for about fifteen minutes before Rednose's phone began to ring. He answered and spoke in a low voice. This made Nya roll her eyes. She could hear Cee Money's voice.

"Who is she, and don't lie because I could hear a girl's voice?" Nya folded her arms, waiting on an answer.

"It was my baby mother. I came here with her and her baby sister. They are having trouble deciding if they are going to visit the beach or the zoo tomorrow before we leave," Rednose admitted without hesitation.

Nya knew she had competition and had to eliminate any competitor that came in the way of her plans. She had chosen Rednose to help her get over her crazy ex-boyfriend, Tyler, and to help her escape her uncle, Rui Sanders, and this lifestyle. When Nya chose a guy, he was hers, and there was no way around it. So, unfortunately for the two ladies that came to her city, this would be their last vacation.

"Tell them to pick the zoo. My family owns most of it, so I can hook you guys up with an exclusive tour that the girls would never forget." Nya was grinning in a cute but very evil way that Rednose failed to pick up on. Also, she was already texting the security at the zoo, telling them that two more girls from out of state would become the next victims.

Chapter 17

Devin had emptied out the driver's trunk and counted all the bags of money by himself. It was less than $100,000. That was when he realized that the driver had pulled a fast break play on him. He must've dropped some money off at a family member's home.

Mad at himself, he sped back to the apartment in Big Quan's car with his big afro blowing in the wind. He had the metal bat wrapped in barbed wire in his hand, ready to beat the driver to death. Nobody was there. All he saw was a big puddle of blood in the middle of the living room and what looked like an eyeball.

"What the fuck did Coby retarded ass do to him? I hope he did not kill the bastard. I was so worried about securing the money. I wasn't thinking about keeping my eyes on Coby's crazy ass! Shit!" Devin yelled to himself as he swung the bat at the night light next to the couch.

He didn't realize that Coby had went all out on the driver. He was so excited about the bags of cash he had discovered in the trunk that he had lost focus. Not only that, but the driver had also cuffed at least half the cash somewhere. Devin had to find out where, so he could get his hands on it. Without the money, he would not be able to run the RRG gang. The members were all hungry for money and didn't respect anything but cash.

Devin got back inside the Benz and sped away. He had dropped off the driver's girl at one of the houses off Clover

Lane. He would have to turn her into a dick sucking machine, so she could pay back some of the money her boyfriend had escaped with. He would tie her up again and force her to cooperate and give up the driver's name and places she knew he had relatives. But first, he needed to talk to Coby to make sure the man was still alive.

All of a sudden, Devin's phone started ringing. It was one of his soldiers. He started not to answer but had a feeling it was important.

"Yo, speak!" Devin yelled at the phone out of frustration.

"Devin, you have to come see this, man. it's like this nigga playing mind games with us. Pull up at the old Walmart parking lot where Big Quan was killed at," the soldier told him before hanging up.

Devin's afro was blowing in the wind as he drove the vehicle like it was a sports car. He knew he couldn't get locked up for a traffic ticket now because Big Quan was gone. Big Quan was a Mason, so the cops used to give him a lot of freedom in the city, but those days were long gone now.

When Devin got to the parking lot, he could not believe what he saw. It was so big that he saw it before he even got on the property.

It was in big, bold, air brushed letters. "Now Who Hiding?" Rednose had counterpunched again.

Devin started punching the air as he drove away. He was so ashamed that he didn't even stop to speak to the small group of RRG members posted around the letters looking stupid, like Rednose was about to drop out the sky.

Devin's phone started ringing again, and this time, it was Coby. He was ready to say fuck using Coby to bait Rednose and Cee Money into a trap. His original plan was to brainwash Coby and fill his memory gaps with lies and deception. Once he was functioning again, he would use him to call Rednose and act like he didn't remember who shot him. Today was the day to use his pawn he had saved. The only reason he saved him was because he needed something to use again Rednose. Coby's condition had not improved over the last six months, so he didn't think he was smart enough to convince Rednose that he wasn't a scam.

This was why Devin had produced the *Stop Hiding* video, just to show Rednose that Coby was alive. Even though he had murdered Cee Money's brother, Randy, with the blow torch, nobody could see any faces or tell Coby was inside the van.

Devin knew he had to do something, and now was the time. So, he answered the call, about to get Coby's small mind ready for what was about to happen, but instead, Coby was the one to shock him.

"I'm at the-the training gym. Red-Rednose was just at my sister's graveyard," Coby said in his retarded speech.

"Hold up, what? Wait, what you just said?" Devin had to make sure he'd heard Coby correctly. He was the only one who could understand Coby's way of talking.

"The picture you-you been showing me. The-the one that killed my sister. He at her graveyard no-now! My girl-girlfriend just called and-and told me." Coby was crying as he spoke, so Devin knew he wasn't lying.

Devin had let Coby see a picture of his sister, Ebony's obituary each day, followed by a picture of Rednose, and worked hard to brainwash Coby into believing that Rednose killed his sister and tried to kill him, but Devin had saved his life.

"Where are you, the gym? Okay, I'm on my way. Stay there. I'll be there in about seven minutes," Devin said before he got off the phone.

Devin got back on the highway because he didn't want to speed through traffic with all the bags of cash inside the Benz. If Rednose was at the cemetery seeing Ebony, that meant Cee Money was there seeing Randy.

Devin would finally get the revenge he'd been craving. He would kill all three of them —Rednose, Cee Money, and

Coby. He would dedicate their dead bodies to Ice Water, Carlos, and Big Quan. He would smoke three blunts of opp pack. Finally, he could smoke on his dead opposition.

Devin noticed that all the lights were off in the training room and just shook his head and jumped out the vehicle.

"Stupid ass, retarded nigga already can't see that good with one eye, but he want to work out in the dark." Devin laughed to himself.

As soon as Devin walked inside the gym, he turned on the lights. It took a few moments for his eyes to adjust to the bright overhead lights. He thought he was tripping when he saw the barrel of a gun pointed at his face.

"Don't reach for it, my G. Pussy boi, keep your hands up and don't move. What, you surprised? You thought I was retarded, nigga. You thought I was still taking that dope you was feeding me a few months ago. Nah, you the retard! I been tricking you. Big, strong, dumb ass pussy nigga, the joke on you!" Coby smiled and started walking normally. He had been moving with a phony limp.

Devin was absolutely speechless. So, Coby kept talking. "Keep your hands up and take me outside to the car where the rest of Big Quan money at! I got the other stash that the driver kept from your smart ass. Oh, you didn't think I would double back and kidnap his ass until he gave up the cash? Fooled you again, motherfucker! This is a stick-up, nigga. You are being robbed. Rednose taught me how to rob a fuck nigga a long time ago. Now hurry the fuck up!"

Coby forced Devin to the van, but when they got outside, something unexpected happened. Two police cars could be heard approaching in the distance. Coby made the mistake of looking back at the cop cars to see how far they were. This gave Devin time to swing his huge fist at Coby. The hit caught Coby off guard, and his gun flew out of his hand.

Devin ran to the other side of the Benz to get his own gun. He had made the mistake of leaving it on the driver's seat. At the same time, Coby had regrouped and picked his gun back up. The two of them approached each other, aiming their guns. It was a standoff.

"Let's do it!" Devin yelled, now back to being the aggressor.

"Shoot, pussy, stop capping!" Coby replied.

They both had a gun to each other's skull. But the police cars were getting closer. Someone must've called the cops when Coby first came to the gym with the bag of money he'd gotten from Big Quan's driver. So, if either one of them shot the other, the police would get directly behind the survivor and chase him for murder. So, they just stared each other down with malice in their eyes.

"I'll see your bitch ass around!" Devin yelled as he started taking steps backwards while still pointing his gun at Coby.

"I'm not doing no hiding, pussy! If you really want to shoot it out, meet me at the cemetery where my sister was buried at. Your uncle, Ice Water, got her killed, nigga!" Coby yelled with tears in his eyes. Devin just smiled. Deep down, he knew that Coby was ready to die.

They both got in different vehicles and went separate ways. The two police cars didn't know which car to chase after. Half of Big Quan's money was with Coby, and the other half was with Devin. One of the cop cars got behind Devin, and the other one got behind Coby.

Halftime.

To Be Continued…

Lock Down Publications and Ca$h Presents
Assisted Publishing Packages

Due to an increase in the price of services we have increased our prices. The prices below reflect the price increase as of 11/1/24.

BASIC PACKAGE $699	UPGRADED PACKAGE $1000
Editing Cover Design Formatting	Typing Editing Cover Design Formatting Upload eBooks to Amazon Upload Paperback to Amazon
ADVANCE PACKAGE $1,400	**LDP SUPREME PACKAGE $1,700**
Typing Editing (line editing/content) Cover Design Formatting Copyright Registration Proofreading Upload eBooks to Amazon Upload Paperback to Amazon	Typing Editing (line editing/content) Cover Design Formatting Copyright Registration Proofreading Set up Amazon Account Upload eBooks to Amazon Upload Paperback to Amazon Advertise on LDP's Amazon and Facebook Page

***Other services available upon request.
Additional charges may apply

Lock Down Publications
P.O. Box 944
Stockbridge, GA 30281-9998
Phone: 470 303-9761
Email: lockdownpublications@gmail.com

Submission Guideline

Submit the first three chapters of your completed manuscript to ldpsubmissions@gmail.com. In the subject line add **Your Book's Title**. The manuscript must be in a Word Doc file and sent as an attachment. Document should be in Times New Roman, double spaced, and in size 12 font. Also, provide your synopsis and full contact information. If sending multiple submissions, they must each be in a separate email.

Have a story but no way to send it electronically? You can still submit to LDP/Ca$h Presents. Send in the first three chapters, written or typed, of your completed manuscript to:

LDP: Submissions Dept
P.O. Box 944
Stockbridge, GA 30281-9998

DO NOT send original manuscript. Must be a duplicate.
Provide your synopsis and a cover letter containing your full contact information.

Thanks for considering LDP and Ca$h Presents.

NEW RELEASES

BLOODLINE OF A SAVAGE 1&2
THESE VICIOUS STREETS 1&2
RELENTLESS GOON
RELENTLESS GOON 2
BY PRINCE A. TAUHID

THE BUTTERFLY MAFIA 1-3
BY FUMIYA PAYNE

A THUG'S STREET PRINCESS 1&2
BY MEESHA

CITY OF SMOKE 2
BY MOLOTTI

STEPPERS 1,2&3
THE REAL BADDIES OF CHI-RAQ
BY KING RIO

THE LANE 1&2
BY KEN-KEN SPENCE

THUG OF SPADES 1&2
LOVE IN THE TRENCHES 2
CORNER BOYS
BY COREY ROBINSON

TIL DEATH 3
BY ARYANNA

THE BIRTH OF A GANGSTER 4
BY DELMONT PLAYER

PRODUCT OF THE STREETS 1&2
BY DEMOND "MONEY" ANDERSON

NO TIME FOR ERROR
BY KEESE

MONEY HUNGRY DEMONS
BY TRANAY ADAMS

Coming Soon from Lock Down Publications/Ca$h Presents

IF YOU CROSS ME ONCE 6
ANGEL V
By Anthony Fields

IMMA DIE BOUT MINE 5
By Aryanna

A THUGS STREET PRINCESS 3
By Meesha

PRODUCT OF THE STREETS 3
By Demond Money Anderson

CORNER BOYS 2
By Corey Robinson

THE MURDER QUEENS 6&7
By Michael Gallon

CITY OF SMOKE 3
By Molotti

CONFESSIONS OF A DOPE BOY
By Nicholas Lock

THA TAKEOVER
By Keith Chandler

BETRAYAL OF A G 2
By Ray Vinci

CRIME BOSS
By Playa Ray

Available Now

RESTRAINING ORDER 1 & 2
By **CA$H & Coffee**

LOVE KNOWS NO BOUNDARIES 1-3
By **Coffee**

RAISED AS A GOON I, II, III & IV
BRED BY THE SLUMS I, II, III
BLAST FOR ME I & II
ROTTEN TO THE CORE I II III
A BRONX TALE I, II, III
DUFFLE BAG CARTEL I II III IV V VI
HEARTLESS GOON I II III IV V
A SAVAGE DOPEBOY I II
DRUG LORDS I II III
CUTTHROAT MAFIA I II
KING OF THE TRENCHES
By **Ghost**

LAY IT DOWN I & II
LAST OF A DYING BREED I II
BLOOD STAINS OF A SHOTTA I & II III
By **Jamaica**

LOYAL TO THE GAME I II III
LIFE OF SIN I, II III
By **TJ & Jelissa**

IF LOVING HIM IS WRONG…I & II
LOVE ME EVEN WHEN IT HURTS I II III
By **Jelissa**

PUSH IT TO THE LIMIT
By **Bre' Hayes**

BLOODY COMMAS I & II
SKI MASK CARTEL I, II & III
KING OF NEW YORK I II, III IV V
RISE TO POWER I II III
COKE KINGS I II III IV V
BORN HEARTLESS I II III IV
KING OF THE TRAP I II
By **T.J. Edwards**

WHEN THE STREETS CLAP BACK I & II III
THE HEART OF A SAVAGE I II III IV
MONEY MAFIA I II
LOYAL TO THE SOIL I II III
By **Jibril Williams**

A DISTINGUISHED THUG STOLE MY HEART I II & III
LOVE SHOULDN'T HURT I II III IV
RENEGADE BOYS 1-4
PAID IN KARMA 1-3
SAVAGE STORMS 1-3
AN UNFORESEEN LOVE 1-3
BABY, I'M WINTERTIME COLD 1-3
A THUG'S STREET PRINCESS 1&2
By **Meesha**

A GANGSTER'S CODE 1-3
A GANGSTER'S SYN 1-3
THE SAVAGE LIFE 1-3
CHAINED TO THE STREETS 1-3
BLOOD ON THE MONEY 1-3
A GANGSTA'S PAIN 1-3
BEAUTIFUL LIES AND UGLY TRUTHS
CHURCH IN THESE STREETS
By **J-Blunt**

CUM FOR ME 1-8
An LDP Erotica Collaboration

BLOOD OF A BOSS 1-5
SHADOWS OF THE GAME
TRAP BASTARD
By **Askari**

THE STREETS BLEED MURDER 1-3
THE HEART OF A GANGSTA 1-3
By **Jerry Jackson**

WHEN A GOOD GIRL GOES BAD
By **Adrienne**

THE COST OF LOYALTY 1-3
By **Kweli**

BRIDE OF A HUSTLA 1-3
THE FETTI GIRLS 1-3
CORRUPTED BY A GANGSTA 1-4
BLINDED BY HIS LOVE
THE PRICE YOU PAY FOR LOVE 1-3
DOPE GIRL MAGIC 1-3
By **Destiny Skai**

A KINGPIN'S AMBITION
A KINGPIN'S AMBITION II
I MURDER FOR THE DOUGH
By **Ambitious**

TRUE SAVAGE 1-7
DOPE BOY MAGIC 1-3
MIDNIGHT CARTEL 1-3
CITY OF KINGZ 1&2
NIGHTMARE ON SILENT AVE
THE PLUG OF LIL MEXICO 1&2
CLASSIC CITY
By **Chris Green**

A GANGSTER'S REVENGE 1-4
THE BOSS MAN'S DAUGHTERS 1-5
A SAVAGE LOVE 1&2
BAE BELONGS TO ME 1&2
A HUSTLER'S DECEIT 1-3
WHAT BAD BITCHES DO 1-3
SOUL OF A MONSTER 1-3
KILL ZONE
A DOPE BOY'S QUEEN 1-3
TIL DEATH 1-3
IMMA DIE BOUT MINE 1-4
By **Aryanna**

A DOPEBOY'S PRAYER
By **Eddie "Wolf" Lee**

THE KING CARTEL 1-3
By **Frank Gresham**

THESE NIGGAS AIN'T LOYAL 1-3
By **Nikki Tee**

GANGSTA SHYT 1-3
By **CATO**

THE ULTIMATE BETRAYAL
By **Phoenix**

BOSS'N UP 1-3
By **Royal Nicole**

I LOVE YOU TO DEATH
By **Destiny J**

I RIDE FOR MY HITTA
I STILL RIDE FOR MY HITTA
By **Misty Holt**

LOVE & CHASIN' PAPER
By **Qay Crockett**

TO DIE IN VAIN
SINS OF A HUSTLA
By **ASAD**

BROOKLYN HUSTLAZ
By **Boogsy Morina**

BROOKLYN ON LOCK 1 & 2
By **Sonovia**

GANGSTA CITY
By **Teddy Duke**

A DRUG KING AND HIS DIAMOND 1-3
A DOPEMAN'S RICHES
HER MAN, MINE'S TOO 1&2
CASH MONEY HO'S
THE WIFEY I USED TO BE 1&2
PRETTY GIRLS DO NASTY THINGS
By **Nicole Goosby**

LIPSTICK KILLAH 1-3
CRIME OF PASSION 1-3
FRIEND OR FOE 1-3
By **Mimi**

TRAPHOUSE KING 1-3
KINGPIN KILLAZ 1-3
STREET KINGS 1&2
PAID IN BLOOD 1&2
CARTEL KILLAZ 1-3
DOPE GODS 1&2
By **Hood Rich**

THE STREETS ARE CALLING
By **Duquie Wilson**

STEADY MOBBN' 1-3
THE STREETS STAINED MY SOUL 1-3
By **Marcellus Allen**

WHO SHOT YA 1-3
SON OF A DOPE FIEND 1-4
HEAVEN GOT A GHETTO 1&2
SKI MASK MONEY 1&2
By **Renta**

GORILLAZ IN THE BAY 1-4
TEARS OF A GANGSTA 1/&2
3X KRAZY 1&2
STRAIGHT BEAST MODE 1&2
By **DE'KARI**

TRIGGADALE 1-3
MURDA WAS THE CASE 1-3
By **Elijah R. Freeman**

SLAUGHTER GANG 1-3
RUTHLESS HEART 1-3
By **Willie Slaughter**

GOD BLESS THE TRAPPERS 1-3
THESE SCANDALOUS STREETS 1-3
FEAR MY GANGSTA 1-5
THESE STREETS DON'T LOVE NOBODY 1-2
BURY ME A G 1-5
A GANGSTA'S EMPIRE 1-4
THE DOPEMAN'S BODYGAURD 1&2
THE REALEST KILLAZ 1-3
THE LAST OF THE OGS 1-3
By **Tranay Adams**

MARRIED TO A BOSS 1-3
By **Destiny Skai & Chris Green**

KINGZ OF THE GAME 1-7
CRIME BOSS 1-3
By **Playa Ray**

FUK SHYT
By **Blakk Diamond**

DON'T F#CK WITH MY HEART 1&2
By **Linnea**

ADDICTED TO THE DRAMA 1-3
IN THE ARM OF HIS BOSS
By **Jamila**

LOYALTY AIN'T PROMISED 1&2
By **Keith Williams**

YAYO 1-4
A SHOOTER'S AMBITION 1&2
BRED IN THE GAME
By **S. Allen**

TRAP GOD 1-3
RICH $AVAGE 1-3
MONEY IN THE GRAVE 1-3
CARTEL MONEY
By **Martell Troublesome Bolden**

FOREVER GANGSTA 1&2
GLOCKS ON SATIN SHEETS 1&2
By **Adrian Dulan**

TOE TAGZ 1-4
LEVELS TO THIS SHYT 1&2
IT'S JUST ME AND YOU
By **Ah'Million**

HUNGRY FOR MONEY | SLIMBOS

KINGPIN DREAMS 1-3
RAN OFF ON DA PLUG
By **Paper Boi Rari**

THE STREETS MADE ME 1-3
By **Larry D. Wright**

CONFESSIONS OF A GANGSTA 1-4
CONFESSIONS OF A JACKBOY 1-3
CONFESSIONS OF A HITMAN
By **Nicholas Lock**

I'M NOTHING WITHOUT HIS LOVE
SINS OF A THUG
TO THE THUG I LOVED BEFORE
A GANGSTA SAVED XMAS
IN A HUSTLER I TRUST
By **Monet Dragun**

QUIET MONEY 1-3
THUG LIFE 1-3
EXTENDED CLIP 1&2
A GANGSTA'S PARADISE
By **Trai'Quan**

CAUGHT UP IN THE LIFE 1-3
THE STREETS NEVER LET GO 1-3
By **Robert Baptiste**

NEW TO THE GAME 1-3
MONEY, MURDER & MEMORIES 1-3
By **Malik D. Rice**

CREAM 2-3
THE STREETS WILL TALK
By **Yolanda Moore**

THE STREETS WILL NEVER CLOSE 1-3
By **K'ajji**

LIFE OF A SAVAGE 1-4
A GANGSTA'S QUR'AN 1-4
MURDA SEASON 1-3
GANGLAND CARTEL 1-3
CHI'RAQ GANGSTAS 1-4
KILLERS ON ELM STREET 1-3
JACK BOYZ N DA BRONX 1-3
A DOPEBOY'S DREAM 1-3
JACK BOYS VS DOPE BOYS 1-3
COKE GIRLZ
COKE BOYS
SOSA GANG 1&2
BRONX SAVAGES
BODYMORE KINGPINS
BLOOD OF A GOON
By **Romell Tukes**

CONCRETE KILLA 1-3
VICIOUS LOYALTY 1-3
By **Kingpen**

THE ULTIMATE SACRIFICE 1-6
KHADIFI
IF YOU CROSS ME ONCE 1-3
ANGEL 1-4
IN THE BLINK OF AN EYE
By **Anthony Fields**

THE LIFE OF A HOOD STAR
By **Ca$h & Rashia Wilson**

NIGHTMARES OF A HUSTLA 1-3
BLOOD AND GAMES 1&2
By **King Dream**

GHOST MOB
By **Stilloan Robinson**

HARD AND RUTHLESS 1&2
MOB TOWN 251
THE BILLIONAIRE BENTLEYS 1-3
REAL G'S MOVE IN SILENCE
By **Von Diesel**

MOB TIES 1-7
SOUL OF A HUSTLER, HEART OF A KILLER 1-3
GORILLAZ IN THE TRENCHES
By **SayNoMore**

BODYMORE MURDERLAND 1-3
THE BIRTH OF A GANGSTER 1-4
By **Delmont Player**

FOR THE LOVE OF A BOSS 1&2
By **C. D. Blue**

KILLA KOUNTY 1-5
By **Khufu**

MOBBED UP 1-4
THE BRICK MAN 1-5
THE COCAINE PRINCESS 1-10
STEPPERS 1-3
SUPER GREMLIN 1-4
By **King Rio**

MONEY GAME 1&2
By **Smoove Dolla**

A GANGSTA'S KARMA 1-4
By **FLAME**

KING OF THE TRENCHES 1-3
By **GHOST & TRANAY ADAMS**

HUNGRY FOR MONEY | SLIMBOS

QUEEN OF THE ZOO 1&2
By **Black Migo**

GRIMEY WAYS 1-3
BETRAYAL OF A G
By **Ray Vinci**

XMAS WITH AN ATL SHOOTER
By **Ca$h & Destiny Skai**

KING KILLA 1&2
By **Vincent "Vitto" Holloway**

BETRAYAL OF A THUG 1&2
By **Fre$h**

THE MURDER QUEENS 1-5
By **Michael Gallon**

FOR THE LOVE OF BLOOD 1-4
By **Jamel Mitchell**

HOOD CONSIGLIERE 1&2
NO TIME FOR ERROR
By **Keese**

PROTÉGÉ OF A LEGEND 1&2
LOVE IN THE TRENCHES 1&2
By **Corey Robinson**

THE PLUG'S RUTHLESS DAUGHTER
By **Tony Daniels**

BORN IN THE GRAVE 1-3
CRIME PAYS
By **Self Made Tay**

MOAN IN MY MOUTH
By **XTASY**

TORN BETWEEN A GANGSTER AND A GENTLEMAN
By **J-BLUNT & Miss Kim**

LOYALTY IS EVERYTHING 1-3
CITY OF SMOKE 1&2
By **Molotti**

HERE TODAY GONE TOMORROW 1&2
By **Fly Rock**

WOMEN LIE MEN LIE 1-4
FIFTY SHADES OF SNOW 1-3
STACK BEFORE YOU SPLURGE
GIRLS FALL LIKE DOMINOES
NAÏVE TO THE STREETS
By **ROY MILLIGAN**

PILLOW PRINCESS
By **S. Hawkins**

THE BUTTERFLY MAFIA 1-3
SALUTE MY SAVAGERY 1&2
By **Fumiya Payne**

THE LANE 1&2
By **Ken-Ken Spence**

THE PUSSY TRAP 1-5
By **Nene Capri**

DIRTY DNA
By **Blaque**

SANCTIFIED AND HORNY
by **XTASY**

BOOKS BY LDP'S CEO, CA$H

TRUST IN NO MAN
TRUST IN NO MAN 2
TRUST IN NO MAN 3
BONDED BY BLOOD
SHORTY GOT A THUG
THUGS CRY
THUGS CRY 2
THUGS CRY 3
TRUST NO BITCH
TRUST NO BITCH 2
TRUST NO BITCH 3
TIL MY CASKET DROPS
RESTRAINING ORDER
RESTRAINING ORDER 2
IN LOVE WITH A CONVICT
LIFE OF A HOOD STAR
XMAS WITH AN ATL SHOOTER

www.ingramcontent.com/pod-product-compliance
Lightning Source LLC
Chambersburg PA
CBHW060424260626
47161CB00005B/1772